ROSS DANE

Aksel Sandemose

Gunnars & Campbell Publishing

GUNNARS & CAMPBELL EDITION

Copyright © 1989

Translated by Christopher Hale

Printed and published in Canada by: Gunnars & Campbell Publishers, 353 Langside Street, Winnipeg, Manitoba Canada R3B 2T3

Cover: H. Vallittu

Printed in Canada

First English Printing: January, 1989

Canadian Cataloguing in Publication Data

Sandemose, Aksel, 1899-1965
      Ross Dane

           Translated from the Norwegian
           ISBN 0-920521-06-1

I. Title
PT8950.S23R613 1989   839.82'3'72 C89-098040-3

61, /26

Funding for this book was provided in part by a grant from the Alberta Heritage Fund.

Introduction

Aksel Sandemose is considered by most Nordic scholars to be one of the leading Scandinavian authors of the mid-twentieth century. His novels are widely read in Scandinavia, and it is impossible to get through high school there without having read at least one of them. In addition he is required reading at most universities where Scandinavian languages and literatures are taught. A number of his works have been translated into English, French, German, Polish and Czech. Unfortunately in spite of this he still remains little known in North America.

He was born March 19, 1899 in Nykøbing, a town on the island of Mors in Jutland, Denmark. His father, Jørgen Nielsen, was a smith, and his mother, Amalie Jakobsdatter, was a Norwegian who had family living on a farm called Sandermosen, the name which Aksel as a young man adopted in a slightly variant form. She had nine children, seven boys and two girls. Aksel was the second youngest. Though not impoverished by the standards of the day, the Nielsen family had to be very careful with money, and this frugality was an everyday fact of life. Because of the long working hours of the father and the almost impossible task of the mother to keep house on the meagre family salary, there was little time left over for being with the children and taking part in their interests and problems. The children, thus, had to be much on their own, and Aksel, as the youngest boy, often suffered the teasing and tormenting of his brothers. As an escape Aksel spent a lot of his boyhood in the countryside around Nykøbing, and perhaps it was during these early wanderings that he developed the perception of drama in nature that gives so much background vitality and eloquence to his novels.

For most working class children of Denmark in the years before World War I, growing up was not easy. The social divisions in society were rigidly adhered to. Usually only the rich were able to go to the school which prepared them for university or for a career. The poor got a less satisfactory education and ordinarily, like young Aksel Sandemose, had to hold down a part-time job as well in order to supplement the family income. In addition schools such as the one he attended tried to imprint on the working class the notion that this discriminatory state of affairs was the natural order of things. Teachers were strict in emphasizing this dictum. All this eventually led to a rebellious attitude. In Aksel's case this developed into a rebellion not so much against society as against the grown-ups and later against the moral and ethical standards of his contemporaries. For the rest of his life Sandemose had to struggle against a feeling of suppression.

After being confirmed at the age of fourteen, Aksel spent a time proving his manhood by taking to drink. But before turning into a real alcoholic, he had himself enrolled in a part-time teacher's school at Staby, near the town of Ringkøbing. The main long term profit Sandemose got out of this schooling was an interest in language and its analysis. In the fall of 1915 he received his certificate as a part time teacher.

No doubt due partially at least to a desire to escape the circumstances of life in small town Denmark and get away from it all, Aksel hired on board the Swedish brigantine *Ragnar af Gefle* toward the beginning of spring, 1916 as an ordinary seaman. His first trip took him to the German city of Stettin and back. Shortly thereafter in the middle of May he signed on with the crew of the Marstal schooner *Katrine* on a trip to Newfoundland via Iceland. Growing dissatisfied with the life of a sailor, one night, late in October, near the island of Fogo, he jumped ship. After a few weeks in Joe Batt's Arm he went over to Newfoundland proper and joined up with a crew of lumberjacks on their way to Campbell's Camp. However, by the beginning of 1917, loaded with guilt feelings about having jumped ship and getting sick of the restrictive and isolated life of the lumbering camp, he went to St. John's. Here he signed on with the crew of the Danish schooner *Chr. H. Rasmussen* to Lisbon and eventually to Spain where he experienced life in the seamier quarters of Cartagena and Ibiza; then on to the Faroe Islands before finally arriving in Denmark in late summer.

On returning to his family home in Nykøbing and spending some time there, he still felt that the town was as oppressive as it had ever been. Finally in 1919 he moved to Copenhagen, enrolling in Døckers Kursus in order to prepare himself for taking the university entrance examination. Here he was able to make friends with others who held interests similar to his own and with whom he could discuss such things as politics, art and literature.

Already while at sea Sandemose had kept a diary, and though he seems not to have read too much as a youth since books were few in his home, he probably became acquainted with the Norwegian author Bjørnstjerne Bjørnson and the Icelandic sagas at a fairly early age. At the school in Staby he read many of the works of the Swedish playwright August Strindberg, and in the spring of 1919 he submitted the manuscript of a book to a small publishing house. This was refused, however, as were other subsequent manuscripts. During these first years in Copenhagen he also discovered, among others, the writings of the melancholy, brooding Norwegian poet Sigbjørn Obstfelder. The first work of Sandemose's actually to appear in print was a prose sketch entitled "Homeless Birds" which came out in the newspaper *Morsø Folkeblad* for July 2, 1921, and concerns a sailor's return home and subsequent departure. Also during December of the same year he contributed several sketches to the newly founded but short lived periodical *Folkerevyen Scandia*.

These years in Copenhagen were hard ones for Sandemose. Economic times were bad, and he had no fixed income. At the end of 1921 he acquired a wife, Dagmar Ditlevsen, a girl from his home town. In April she gave birth to twins, Hedda and Eva, putting an even greater strain on Aksel's financial situation. Shortly thereafter he returned to Nykøbing, the place he had so longed to get away from, in order to find work. Holding a job as colporteur he spent all the free time he could in writing, and finally at the beginning of 1923 he was able to get a short story printed in the newly established periodical *Forum*. The man who had founded this publication was the then well-established and acclaimed Danish author Johannes V. Jensen. Jensen recognized Sandemose's talent and used his influence to help get his first book, *Stories from Labrador*, published with the prestigious Copenhagen firm of Gyldendal. It appeared on November 7, 1923. Aksel was twenty-four.

Though he had at this time never been to Labrador, his debut book consisted of eleven short tales about hunters, sailors and loggers with that harsh land as a backdrop. It was well received by the critics. The following year, 1924, saw the publication of three more of his books: *Storms at Equinox*, *Sin of Youth* and *Men from the Atlantic*. *Storms at Equinox* is actually two short stories. The first one, "The Man from the Cave", depicts a former seaman who settles down on shore, but tries to escape the restrictions of society by spending almost all his free time in a cave he digs for himself out in the forest. The protagonist of the second story, "In the Corridor of Life", actively takes a stand against the society he lives in and eventually triumphs over it. Both *Sin of Youth* and *Men from the Atlantic* are essentially sea stories, full of action, but with somewhat artificially constructed plots and melodramatic situations. Yet there are powerful scenes, especially those which describe sailing ships in storms at sea.

Most of the contemporary criticism of these three works was negative, and as a result Sandemose became quite depressed; nearly three years passed before another novel appeared. It became more and more difficult for him to provide for his family, and he was virtually on the point of giving up writing as a profession. By the beginning of 1925 his circumstances forced him to take a job as a guard at the Ny Carlsberg Glyptotek in Copenhagen, a position he held for two years. In addition he was appointed editor of a local newspaper, *Hareskov Grundejerblad*, and this must have helped him at least somewhat to overcome the feelings of degradation over his Glyptotek job. He did keep on writing, though, during these years, mostly articles, essays and short stories for various newspapers and periodicals as well as a couple of novels. The novels were, however, rejected. Finally he had a success in *The Klabautermann which was published in March, 1927. This novel has as its motif the myth of the phantom seaman whose appearance signals a watery death for those who see him.*

The mid-1920's was a time when emigration was a favourite topic of discussion in Denmark as elsewhere. The U.S. Immigration Act of 1924 had virtually cut off the stream of immigrants to that country, and this left Canada as the only place in North America still readily open to them. In July, 1927 Sandemose reviewed a book by the editor Chr. Mikkelsen who the year before had visited western Canada. He had returned extolling the virtues of the country and urging those who were interested to try out a life there. Since Sandemose, because of his Newfoundland experiences, was interested in Canada, this book may have whetted his appetite to see things for himself. Furthermore he probably just wanted to get away from Denmark for a while, because of his poor economic situation and uncertain future. Luckily he was able to get one of the leading Copenhagen newspapers, *Berlingske Tidende*, to hire him as a "special correspondent" to send back articles on various facets of life and nature in the country. As well, the Canadian Pacific Railway paid his travel expenses, since the company was interested in making Canada known to prospective immigrants. He also kept a detailed diary while abroad.

On August 10, 1927 Sandemose sailed from Denmark, reaching Quebec City on August 20. Continuing on via Montreal, Toronto and Erie, Pennsylvania, he arrived in Winnipeg, the gateway to the Canadian prairies on September 9. Winnipeg at the time was a city full of immigrants from all over the world, and one thing that struck Sandemose especially here was the immigrant who had failed in farm work and had returned to town to become a beggar and a derelict. But Sandemose wanted to see what the countryside was like and so continued west, following a route similar to the one Chr. Mikkelsen had traversed the previous year. On September 12 he reached the town of Maryfield, just over the border from Manitoba in Saskatchewan. After acquiring a horse and riding around on the prairie for several days, he returned to Winnipeg.

Redvers, Saskatchewan is the main town in a heavily Danish area which has been known as Dannevirke. Sandemose came to Redvers on September 27 and stayed in the region for 16 days. He visited a number of the farmers in the district, but the one who impressed him most and whom he stayed with briefly was Simon Hjortnæs, a main landholder living near the village of Alida. Hjortnæs was known far and wide as the one to whom Danish immigrants should turn if they ever needed assistance. He had been born in Denmark but at an early age had emigrated with his family to South Dakota. Then as a young man he had moved up across the border into Canada, where he eventually settled. Being essentially the first Dane in the area and encouraging other Danes to join him, he became the leader of the new colony and was frequently referred to as the King of the Danes.

Again taking the train back to Winnipeg on October 13, Sandemose spent the next three weeks wandering around the city, meeting people and making excursions into the surrounding countryside, often to hunt. But by the beginning of November he realized that staying in Winnipeg was fruitless, and so with only a few dollars left of his money, he made his way to the newly formed Danish colony in the area around Holden, Alberta. Winter had already arrived when Sandemose reached Holden on November 5. Staying here with Peter Sorensen, a man whose name had probably been given to him by Simon Hjortnæs, he met local farmers, picked up anecdotes which he confided to his diary and travelled around visiting Beaver Hills, Edmonton and Camrose.

On November 17 Sandemose came to the mining town of Wayne in the Drumheller region of Alberta. On the prairie surrounding the coulee where Wayne is situated is the Danish colony of Dalum. He stopped here for four weeks, again meeting the local Danish population. Among other things he debated religious matters for long hours with the minister of the Dalum congregation, Pastor Rasmussen, gave a lecture on evolution at the minister's home and spent five days isolated by a snowstorm in a shack in East Coulee together with an immigrant named John Andersen. On the whole Sandemose was much impressed with the Dalum community and its Danish high school, and in his later articles he strongly recommends such colonies as goals for the would-be Danish emigrant.

Sandemose left Dalum on December 14 and went to Calgary where he stayed in the Palliser Hotel. He met the Danish consul Mr. Pallesen and Pastor Knudsen and discussed with them the question of Danish immigration to the prairies. Also it was during his stay in Alberta that he began to make notes for a novel to be called *People on the Prairie*.

But Sandemose was running out of money, and as winter was setting in he was becoming more and more homesick. Furthermore, by now he felt that he was not suited to the often harsh and difficult life in prairie Canada, so on December 19 he took the express train directly to Toronto, arriving there on the 22. The next month and a half or so he spent with his sister Anna in Erie,

Pennsylvania, leaving for Denmark on February 10, 1928. Two years later in 1930 Sandemose emigrated from Denmark, not to Canada, but rather to Norway, the original homeland of his mother.

Actually, then, Sandemose spent only three and a half months of his life in western Canada. Yet his diary entries and the several dozen articles he wrote for various Danish newspapers show his keen observation of many phases of life on the prairies. Most important of all, of course, and surprising is the fact that his brief sojourn gave him the material for three novels which are all set in the province of Alberta - *Ross Dane*, *A Sailor Goes Ashore* and *September*. *Ross Dane*, named after the main character in the book, tells the story of a Danish immigrant to Alberta who, with a small group of companions, establishes the colony of Beaver Coulee on the prairie and eventually becomes the leading farmer in the area. *A Sailor Goes Ashore*, published in 1931 and Sandemose's first Norwegian novel, is a sort of sequel to *Ross Dane*. The protagonist, Espen Arnakke, is Sandemose's alter ego. He kills a man in Newfoundland after jumping ship there, and flees to Beaver Coulee where as he adjusts to the harsh conditions of life on the prairie he tries to come to terms with the fact that he is a murderer. *September* (1939) deals with a love triangle and also is concerned with the question of to what extent a first generation immigrant has become a real Canadian or remained a part of the old country.

These three novels in effect constitute a western Canadian trilogy.

Ross Dane appeared in 1928 and was very well received both by the critics and by the reading public. It also proved to be the last novel Sandemose published in Danish, though it was later translated into Norwegian under the title *Settlers in Alberta*. Rasmus Dansker, who in the second part has totally Canadianized his name to Ross Dane, is modelled, as Sandemose readily admitted, on Simon Hjortnæs of Alida, Saskatchewan. Like Simon, Ross first comes to Canada from South Dakota while chasing some runaway horses. Also like Simon, Ross becomes the leading figure in the Danish colony he establishes and is known as King Dane. Much in the character of the two men is similar. But the action has been transferred to Alberta. When describing Beaver Coulee itself, Sandemose undoubtedly had the Wayne/Dalum area in mind, but the nearby town is probably based on Redvers, with a bit of Holden added to it.

The novel in many ways follows in the footsteps of Sandemose's earlier production. One of the things that he had been concerned with was a concept coming out of the world of the Icelandic sagas which he himself had already dealt with in several essays. This is the belief in two main types of human being, translated into Danish as the "lykkemand" and the "nidding" - the man of luck and the man of no luck. The "lykkemand" is born fortunate. Fate smiles on him throughout his life, and he always succeeds in everything he attempts. The "nidding" on the other hand comes into the world without any good fortune. He might be considered a born loser, destined to fail and to remain outside society. In Sandemose's novels from the 1920's the contrast between the "lykkemand" and the "nidding" is almost always present, and usually the "lykkemand" is the hero of the story, the one whom the author seems most to identify with.

Like these heroes, Ross Dane too is a "lykkemand". Everything he sets his mind to succeeds. He is a powerhouse of energy, the ideal immigrant to the Canadian prairie. But the "nidding" is represented also, primarily in the person of Theodor Pedersen. From the moment we meet him in Moose Jaw we see he is doomed.

Some of the finest parts of the book are the descriptions of nature and natural effects - the sunset on the prairie, the wind howling through the strange formations in North Coulee, the prairie fire and the broken bell yelps of the coyotes at night. These and the other such passages paint a vivid picture of the prairie and form a powerful backdrop to the action of the novel. In addition we catch glimpses of what the life of the immigrant was like - the prairie wife doomed to a life of loneliness and depression; the man who has left his family behind in Denmark and is struggling to earn enough money to bring them over; the parasite who sponges off other immigrants in order to survive.

One problem which Sandemose found existing on the prairies and which bothered him considerably was racism. In a number of his articles he complains that western Europeans were especially prone to looking down on eastern Europeans, those which come under the term Galicians and which include people from Poland, Russia, the Ukraine, Bohemia and even Greece. Sandemose could find no real grounds for this prejudice, and in an interview with a reporter from the *Montreal Herald* on his return from the west, he says that he found the Galician to be as good a farm worker as the Scandinavian, if not better. This theme of racism is reflected in *Ross Dane* as well. One of the main villains in the book is Fyodor Murazeszky, a Galician. But as a counterweight to him, and perhaps to avoid having an accusing finger pointed at him, Sandemose makes one of the good characters a Galician also.

Seen in its entirety, *Ross Dane* is a well written book and eminently worth reading. It is full of life, excitement and wit, and it gives the English speaking reader an interesting picture of the way a European saw life on the Canadian prairies a couple of generations ago.

Sandemose's novels after *Ross Dane* became more personal, and the author now delved into his own psyche. He found that rather than being a "lyk-kemand" himself, he was actually a "nidding". His upbringing and the small town environment of his youth had cowed him. Espen Arnakke, who is introduced in *A Sailor Goes Ashore* but who is also the protagonist in other books, most importantly *A Fugitive Crosses his Tracks* from 1933, was raised under similar circumstances. In the latter novel Espen's childhood is explored in order to uncover the reasons why he came to commit a murder later in his life. Most of the blame is placed on Espen's home town of Jante and its moral and ethical standards. During the German occupation of Norway Sandemose was forced to flee his adopted country for Sweden. The central novel to come from his pen during this time was *The Past is a Dream* (1944), portraying the identity crisis of a Norwegian-American. Probably his most important work from the post-war years is *The Werewolf* (1958) which deals again with the "nidding" and his search for his "self". Throughout his life Sandemose wrote articles and essays as well as novels.

Though appreciated in his lifetime as an author of note, since his death in 1965 Aksel Sandemose has been more and more truly recognized as occupying a foremost position among the authors of Scandinavia.

ROSS DANE
First Part
1.

"**H**ey, you! you there! Take *that*, you damned scum!"

Rasmus Dansker wrenched himself around just as a blow struck him hard above the right ear. He plummeted from the top of the railroad car to the gravel and rolled down the embankment into a large bush. Above him the wheels whirled round and round, the whole world whirled around. Toward the front of the train, which now began to pick up speed, a man leaned his whole upper body out of a trapdoor and yelled threats at Rasmus Dansker's broad back sticking out of the bush. A curve in the tracks soon took him out of sight.

Rasmus ran up the escarpment on all fours with gravel rattling behind him. He had exactly enough time to grab on to the end of the last car where there was an iron hoop just large enough for a man who enjoys riding freight trains to sit on.

Cautiously he lifted a hand up and felt his head. God, what a bump! He licked the blood off his gashed lips, sighed, and dried his bloody hands on his trousers. Positioning himself as comfortably as he could on the sharp iron, he thoughtfully sucked his teeth to find out how many were loose, and started to whistle a tune in sad funeral-march tempo as he looked at the receding landscape.

It was a mild, hazy spring day in North Dakota. The train was northbound, not far from the Canadian border which Rasmus intended to cross in order to find the fifty-five horses that a wise Norwegian seer had told him were grazing in a certain valley by the Souris River. A broad smile came over his face as he thought of the man...

Rasmus had come from the south to a little Norwegian settlement while he was looking for those fifty or so runaways that he had invested his entire fortune

1

in; but the Norwegians hadn't seen or heard anything about the Dane's horses. They did tell him about a man living with his grandmother out on the prairie who could divine water. If that was true, thought Rasmus, the fellow could probably divine horses too.

When he went out to see him, only the grandmother was at home. Rasmus waited for him till sunset. The two nodded to each other, but before Rasmus had stated his business or said anything at all, the Norwegian fell into a trance, became blue and yellow in the face, showed the whites of his eyes and whispered hoarsely,

"You are Rasmus Dansker, also known as Ross Dane, and you've been looking for fifty-five horses which are legally yours. They're all in Sunny Valley by the Souris River in Canada. You can pick them up there without paying any ransom money."

The Norwegian had given this information for free, and Rasmus didn't much believe in its accuracy, but he thought he might as well look in the indicated direction as anywhere else. He left the farm laughing aloud as he remembered how the Norwegian's face looked in the throes of prophesying. Rolling a dumpy-looking cigarette, he walked toward the nearest railway line to travel to Sunny Valley in his accustomed manner.

The locomotive was pulling the long freight train northward at a speed of scarcely more than ten miles an hour. In the beginning Rasmus felt a nagging pain in his rear end on account of his narrow seat. A little later his legs began to fall asleep. This was painful, but finally passed into a numbness which gave him the sensation of having artificial legs. He presented a rather comic spectacle holding on firmly with his hands, now and then stretching one stiff arm or the other into the air as if he were admonishing somebody, and his red face caked with patches of dried blood.

The train moved with a melancholy rumble through the deserted countryside. The prairie lay brilliantly green with multicoloured patches of flowers. Dwarf trees stood around the waterholes with hawks circling over them. Rasmus gradually got the feeling that the great open land was just waiting for something...

Suddenly an ominous voice sounded through the clacking of the wheels on the rails:

"So there you are, you son-of-a-bitch! I'll teach you, you damn -"

Though at that moment paralysed in the lower part of his body and in a bad way generally, Rasmus didn't take time to reflect. The voice came from above, but he didn't look to see who shouted. He let himself fall. Something struck the gravel with a heavy thud not half a yard from him. It was a large, twisted piece of iron. From the top of the boxcar a man shouted something or other as the train trundled on.

Rasmus neither heard nor answered. Several hours passed. The shadows began to lengthen. Two black eagles soared in enormous elipses over the railway line. When they came so low that the reflection of the sun could be seen in their eyes, they rose again and disappeared. The man lay on the tracks as if asleep with one of the rails under his neck and his legs curled up under him.

It began to get dark. Still Rasmus lay in the same position.

Ahead of him, far ahead, a new life and a new world seemed to be beginning - a world that was blissfully tremulous, a world where he was one with the universe. There had never been anything else but this sweet, faint trembling.

Slowly he opened his eyes and looked dully up at the stars. He didn't marvel at it. There had never been anything else in the world, nothing but this continual, ever increasing trembling, and then a look that mirrored the starry heavens.

Soon it was like a trembling note which came from without. At other times it was created within him. It came closer, an intensely rising song...

He turned his head. The first thing he became aware of was his own person. Without bending his arm he swung it in an arc over the gravel until his hand struck the rail. He pensively felt the cold iron. The rythmic beat in his head now found its way to his hand. Gripping the rail, he now felt the beat. In the next instant more things passed through Rasmus' mind than otherwise did during a whole day. There wasn't time to stand up, so he drove his feet hard into the flint and flew from the tracks like a bobcat springing. Once more an endless row of wheels whirred past him. He stared up with a sickish feeling at the black freight train as though he had returned from his own execution with his head only loosely put back on his shoulders.

But - the train was headed north. There was no point in hesitating. If only his arms and legs were sound he'd be man enough to board a moving freight train. He got up quickly. He felt sore as hell, sore all over, but he didn't think he had broken anything. He waited, judging the train's length at about a hundred cars. This time maybe he'd be allowed to hang in peace on the last one.

His jump was unsuccessful. And what was worse, he rolled ten yards or so down the stony embankment until he ended up in a swamp. Spattered with water and mud he extricated himself and looked despondently back at the train. "God damn it!" he snarled, and spat out a rotten piece of wood back where it had come from.

His matches were soaking wet, but eventually he got a fire going. Then he ran around gathering wood, managing to keep himself fairly warm until the fire was big and hot. He stretched his blanket between a couple of sticks, and the steam soon drifted like a cloud from both it and him. His bread had not got any tastier from being mixed with swamp water, but it could be eaten as long as he didn't let any light shine on it.

Then Rasmus Dansker lay down and slept the sleep of the righteous.

- - - - -

In the cold dawn he woke up and tried to roll a cigarette, but all his papers were stuck together after his experience in the swamp.

"Here's paper, friend."

Taken aback, Rasmus turned his head. Over on the other side of the now smouldering fire an arm stretched out from a pile of blankets.

"Who the hell are you?"

"I'm on my way to Canada, and my name is Charles Villeneuve. How about you?"

"Well, my name's Rasmus. I thought I was alone."

"I came too late to catch the emigrant express. I see you decided to get off up here. I saw your fire and lay down," the stranger answered.

Rasmus laughed.

"Got off, huh! Well, you see, pal, I was thrown off the morning train and lost my footing when I tried to catch the night train. Otherwise I'd have been in Canada by now. Are you an Indian?"

"Actually I'm a Metis. Indian mother, French-Canadian father. I've been looking for runaway horses down here."

"Ha!" Rasmus laughed. "I'm on my way to Canada on the same business. Hell of a thing. I put all my money into those animals. And then they ran off. Three years ago I put my money into oil, but nothing came up except salt water. Two years before that I was held up by four negroes. I always seem to be lucky. I'm always getting thrown off trains, always hurting myself or rolling into a swamp. It's a stinking world."

Charles nodded seriously. "Yes," he said.

"You're an exceptional fellow," Rasmus said and lay down. "Let's go on together, huh?"

They agreed. A little later when the two got up, Rasmus stared dumbfoundedly at Charles Villeneuve. Rasmus himself was of more than average height, but Charles was a foot and a half taller, and the most well-proportioned man Rasmus had ever seen.

"How - did you get to be so big?"

Charles took the question quite seriously.

4

"There are princes on both my mother's side and my father's."

"You must be pretty damned strong."

"Yes, I'm very strong."

Rasmus stroked his chin, completely astonished.

"Are you all like that up in your neck of the woods?"

"No, the others are small - like you."

"Oh, like me? Well. Now I understand better, friend, why you weren't afraid to lie down by a stranger's campfire out here."

"Oh - you're a peaceful man. You let your fire shine far and wide, and you don't have any weapons. You have no fear. That's why you wouldn't attack anyone who's asleep."

"Look here, I don't attack people asleep or awake. But you say I'm not afraid. Then you should have seen me this evening when I discovered I was about to be run over by a train. You say I have no fear! I jumped like a cockroach. You can bet I was afraid!"

For the first time Charles smiled.

"I wouldn't have rolled up my sleeves either to have a go at a giant locomotive and a hundred and twelve freight cars, even if they were empty. I'd have run for a lot less than that."

"Well, but I was damned scared," said Rasmus.

One on each side, Charles Villeneuve and Rasmus Dansker jumped on the northbound morning freight and situated themselves back to back on an iron suspension leaf under one of the cars. Fourteen hours later up in Canada they sneaked off the train. Rasmus felt as if he had caught a rifle slug in his belly and leaned heavily on Charles. They found lodgings for the night in one of last year's haystacks.

5

2.

Near Estevan, Charles and Rasmus bought themselves horses and a couple of old saddles. They swam over Long Creek, an arm of the Souris River, and rode south along the river's western bank to Sunny Valley. It was still the same quiet, hazy weather it had been for a month now. Charles, who had proof that his horses were down in the States, had given up finding them, but Rasmus did not want to stop looking for his until he had followed the advice of the clairvoyant Norwegian. Charles had given him new hope, as he thought it probable that the Norwegian was right. He told Rasmus in plain words that horses had often been found by means of such information. At last Rasmus became so convinced that he began taking it for granted that his horses could be picked up in Sunny Valley.

They camped at the entrance to the valley on a moonlit night. Rasmus felt sure he would find his horses the next day. During the night he awoke and saw that Charles was gone. He got up and looked for him, but the half-Indian was not to be seen anywhere nearby. He strolled around a bit and finally found him leaning against a tree, smoking a cigarette. As Rasmus approached he lifted his hand holding the cigarette and said,

"Your horses are grazing over there between the hills. They are marked R.D."

Rasmus stood for a while looking in that direction.

"Yes, they're mine," he said, "but it might not be a bad thing if I had been packing one of those six-shooters they carry around in cowboy stories."

Charles smiled.

"Perhaps not," he said, "but you know we have most of the night ahead of us. We can get quite a way with those horses before daybreak."

As much as possible they hid among the bushes as they approached. The stud of horses was very carefully enclosed behind a barbed-wire fence. Gradually the outlines of a house appeared not far away. They stood quietly and looked at it.

"I'll bet we can count on their being asleep," remarked Charles.

7

"It's a pain in the ass," said Rasmus, "for somebody to steal his own horses from a thief in the middle of the night like this."

"It's the simplest way," answered Charles flatly.

Before entering the corral, they saddled up and made everything ready for a quick getaway. They let the horses out and began driving them toward the northwest.

When the sun came up they were twenty miles from Sunny Valley. They didn't stop to rest. Sometimes in front of them, sometimes between them the half wild horses were rushing with dilated nostrils and flying manes. Their tracks showed clearly on the prairie. If anyone took up pursuit, speed was their only chance for safety.

As the sun rose they began more and more often to look behind them, but still there seemed to be no one on their trail.

It became a scorchingly hot day, and the horses began to slow down. Charles and Rasmus took up their ropes. Around noon they reached the Souris River and led the horses into the water for half an hour or so, heading in a southeasterly direction. They left the river on the left bank and set their sights due north until they reached Huntoon. Just north of the settlement they figured they could finally take a rest. The horses were allowed to graze, and the two men delved into the provisions they had in their saddlebags. They agreed to continue on again after half an hour's rest and not to stop until late that night.

"I might just as well become a horsethief," Rasmus said when they again galloped off. "There aren't any boundaries between your own property and other people's. If somebody wants his own horses, he's supposed to steal them just as if he wanted somebody else's."

Charles didn't say anything. He lay leaning over his horse's neck, twirling his long rope above his head. To him horses had never been property in the same way as other earthly goods. In his soul lived the Indian ethos that a horse was a horse. What counted was getting the best possible one. It didn't matter whether you bought it or stole it. Thus he saw nothing shocking in a person's for once having to steal his own horses.

Just after dark one of the best animals in the stud fell down. Charles circled around it and saw that it had broken one of its forelegs in a badger hole. Without stopping, Charles tossed his rifle forward into his right hand like a revolver and shot the crippled horse through its head. Rasmus was furious. When Charles came up alongside him a little later, Rasmus said angrily,

"I'm beginning to get sick of this. Here I'm supposed to chase about like an idiot, and then it turns out that I have to lose a horse as well."

Charles' eyes shone in the moonlight as he rushed ahead. It was clear he felt good. He didn't reply.

Around midnight they struck camp. They took turns standing watch over the horses, an easy chore because the exhausted animals made no attempt to run away.

Soon after sunrise they were again heading north. Rasmus began to take notice of the land. His eye, which was trained to such things, told him that the soil was good. Surely one could get a homestead here for almost nothing. He rode up beside Charles and shouted.

"I'm going to stay in Canada."

"Of course you're going to stay in Canada," said Charles, laughing. "I knew that the moment I saw you. Otherwise why would you be riding north as if the devil were after you? It would have been far safer for you to go back across the border to the States."

They rode for a while in silence. Then Rasmus said calmly,

"Well, I guess I'm meant to stay in Canada dead or alive - because now they're after us."

Charles took a cursory look behind him.

"About ten men," he said.

They rode on for a couple of minutes, then stopped. Since it was clear the pursuers rode fresh horses, they'd have to get out of this jam not by flight but by cunning or force. They decided to let the horses run on, for it would be easy to find their tracks again on the prairie. They themselves would wait for the pursuers.

Fifteen minutes later they were surrounded.

"What are your names, and where do you live?" asked the leader.

Charles didn't say anything, but Rasmus looked around furiously at the strangers and said,

"First I'd like to know what kind of blighters you are."

The leader didn't answer but took some papers out of his saddlebag and held them in front of Rasmus's face.

"I'm the sheriff of Estevan and Sunny Valley," he said curtly. "Last night you robbed the county corral where the stray horses are."

Charles and Rasmus looked at each other. Then Rasmus scratched the back of his neck and said,

"Well, strictly speaking I guess that can't be denied. What did I say, Charles? Haven't I always had the damnedest luck? I speculate in oil, and I get saltwater. I speculate in horses, and they run away. I steal my own horses back, instead of just calmly going off with them."

While he was talking, he pulled out his papers and certified who he was, and that the brand on the horses was his.

The whole affair ended with laughter, but first Rasmus had to hand over money for his horses, and he had to pay a daily wage to the sheriff's men and a fine to the sheriff himself because he had torn a hole in a county corral. Finally they parted, and when Rasmus and Charles again had caught hold of the stud of horses, they struck camp for a couple of days to catch their breath after their fright.

"But that Norwegian fellow was still a liar," Rasmus said, "because I did end up paying a big ransom."

3.

Now Rasmus and Charles agreed to travel westward. Gradually they turned more to the north until they came to Moose Jaw. There Rasmus parted profitably with his horses, earning a fair amount on the deal. He had been prepared after all his trouble to sell for less. Moose Jaw at the time was just a dot on the prairie with a half dozen or so wooden houses. Rasmus had to wait in town almost a week to get his money, and in the meantime Charles wanted to use the opportunity to visit an old relative of his who lived a few miles out of town.

Nothing of any importance was happening in Moose Jaw, and Rasmus, quickly regretting not having made the trip with Charles, suffered from inactivity. Only the odd cowboy travelling through, or an immigrant looking at land, came into the Chinese cafe. Rasmus would hang over the tables with them exchanging a story or two before they went on. The sun shone mercilessly during those long days; inch-wide gaps appeared between the wallboards in the half dozen houses there. The dust rose up in a low cloud wherever he walked. People were almost never to be seen. Early in the year though it was, the prairie grass was being scorched. It lay around one's feet like matted twine. The prairie rose bloomed. A deathly stillness hung over the land. In the evening it cooled down somewhat, and there were noises; a night bird cried, and a coyote yelped somewhere. Then Rasmus began remembering Denmark...

He had spent only his childhood there. When he was nine years old, he journeyed with his parents and brothers and sisters to South Dakota. He continued to be more Danish than many of those who had lived their first twenty-five years in Denmark, because he knew it only as the carefree land of childhood and happiness. He longed for it, but only in the way that one may long for the childhood to which he can never return. Rasmus would just reminisce at those times when others would have read a book or played an accordion.

11

One stiflingly hot day a wagon came to Moose Jaw. Rasmus immediately went to meet it. It was a rough box wagon that clearly unskilled hands had constructed by nailing together various pieces of wood which had been picked up here and there. Only the high, slender wheels were new. The team consisted of a cow, two horses and a donkey. Rasmus stood in the middle of the trail scrutinizing the procession.

"Well I'll be!" he said.

In the wagon sat two little girls and two half-grown boys, and a man of about fifty walked beside it. Rasmus saw at once by their evasive glance that they didn't understand English. He walked closer.

"Are you Germans? New arrivals, huh?"

The older one shook his head.

"Scandinavians?"

"Yes."

"And perhaps Danes to boot!" shouted Rasmus. The others laughed with delight.

They were indeed Danes.

"My God!" yelled Rasmus. "You didn't really come from Halifax with that team?"

"No, no, just from Winnipeg..."

"Oh, *just* from Winnipeg! Why don't you hitch up a cat or a skunk as well. You could make a whole zoo out of it..."

The older man's look became dark.

"Go away!" he said sharply. "We haven't sent for you. There's room enough here without you following us."

For a second it looked as though Rasmus would pounce on the other man. But then his smile came back as he coolly began to roll a cigarette.

"Indeed there is room enough here. As a matter of fact there's too much room," he said at last. "If there were less, probably none of us would be here. Can't you take a joke, pop, huh? Go on and grab your rifle. You won't shoot it!"

The other man had actually made a move toward his weapon. Now he pulled it out.

"Get out of here!" he shouted and pointed the barrel at Rasmus.

"You're a fool," said Rasmus. "But that's the way these people are who have just come to this country; they think we go around over here picking off each other. Ha, as if we were too many! No, old man, we don't kill people here and then get a reputation as stalwart fellows afterward. To begin with we don't kill. And secondly we get arrested and hanged when we do. *That's* the way it is."

The other one looked for an honourable retreat. Like many new people he

12

was ashamed at being caught doing something un-Canadian.

"Why can't I shoot, you conceited ass?" he asked at last.

"Why?" said Rasmus and struck another match on the back of his trousers. "Why? Now really..."

His opponent saw something rise up in the road, but before he could collect himself, he was lying legs up in a tangle of rose bushes, as Rasmus emptied the rifle of bullets.

"You see in this country we take the canon away from people who don't obey the law," he explained. "Come on now and be reasonable so we can laugh a little together at nature. That cow has turned-out feet. It's no good wandering about with a cow, so let's sell her to the Chinaman. Rather do without milk. How far are you going? What are your names?"

"We're all named Pedersen. Maybe I did act stupidly, but you have a brazen way about you."

"My name's Rasmus. I came up from the States to find a stud of horses, and now I'm waiting around here for a friend. We're going northwest, so I can look around a little while I'm here. Where are you going?"

"We're going to Alberta."

Rasmus looked more closely at the man.

"Look, to me you're a hard nut. You're as old as Abraham. So far you've walked straight through Manitoba and a good bit further. So you're going to Alberta. Train tickets aren't really that expensive."

"They've earned enough money off me already," Pedersen interrupted.

The two men exchanged a quick glance, but this time Rasmus didn't say what he was thinking. However, he couldn't completely restrain himself.

"I don't think you were really thinking of treating me to four cents' worth of lead, pop."

"It's easy enough for you single people to talk," Pedersen growled. "When you get responsibility you sing a different tune."

— — —

The Pedersen family made camp outside town, and Rasmus stayed with them the rest of the day. He discovered that Pedersen had been a bailiff on a farm somewhere in Jutland, but had got the idea of going to Canada because he hadn't been able to manage his money matters. Though it hadn't been long since he'd left Denmark, still the old man's great dreams had, one by one, crumbled to dust. It had been a hard trip over the Atlantic. He had never been on the ocean before; its great bright dream had revealed itself as a merciless reality. He had entertained many fine thoughts about how smoothly and

13

wonderfully everything would go when they landed in Canada; but before they left Montreal his wife had died and been buried there. Canada had become a reality, one which it appeared he had by now resigned himself to. He mourned the loss of his wife. Still life could somehow go on without her.

The two little girls looked quite neglected; their faces scarcely ever saw water. Each had two stiff braids sticking straight back, but otherwise looked like typical Jutlandic peasant children. Rasmus felt he had seen them a hundred times before. Of the fourteen and sixteen year old boys, only the youngest resembled his father - to the extent it was possible to discern the old fellow's features behind a bushy reddish beard which reached far down on to his chest. The beard grew wild on his face; around his nose there were large warts with long hairs on them, and his whiskers grew up under his eyes. He had an open, aggressive look; he laughed a lot and liked to shout loudly. Rasmus had from the start been on half friendly and half hostile terms with the man. They spoke laughingly with each other but were mutually on guard. Rasmus kept gibing him because he wanted to walk to Alberta, but Pedersen found a secret respect in the other man's voice and thought that this young, powerful fellow actually could be taken along. Strong hands would be useful out there. At the thought he secretly looked over at his two sons. The youngest - he was good enough; but, God forbid, the oldest, he was certainly not worth much.

Rasmus followed his eyes. Pedersen's oldest son was large for his age but looked as though he travelled with the shadow of death. Rasmus found out that he suffered from tuberculosis. He did not resemble his father at all, for the lines of his face were finer, and his look was intelligent and mild, without his father's stony sarcasm, which there were clear signs of in the younger son's demeanor. Theodor was his name. He seemed not to belong racially to the rest of his family, either. He was a dark, sinewy Galician type.

Rasmus ate with them that evening. The food was potatoes and boiled rabbit meat. When the girls were put to bed and Rasmus was about to go, Pedersen said,

"Such a young and unattached man as you are, somebody who knows this land the way you do, you should join forces with us. Then we'd be a whole colony - out there in Alberta."

Rasmus stood with his feet far apart and looked at him. "Yes," he said, "you're quite right there. But now I think it would be better if you wrote to Denmark and got hold of a woman for that colony. That would be better for the two little girls."

Pedersen looked down.

"You talk," he said.

Rasmus stood for a moment looking at him. Then he said he'd come back

14

tomorrow and went to Moose Jaw.

The next day the Pedersen family made no move to journey on. Rasmus walked around out by their camp part of the day. Nothing was said about Pedersen's proposition. The day after that Pedersen camped at Moose Jaw. He still said nothing more to Rasmus about coming along; he was a man who worked tacitly and could wait.

As far as Rasmus was concerned the whole thing gradually came to depend on Charles Villeneuve. When the idea had first been offered to him, he had thought it would be very funny to trudge along with the Pedersens to Alberta. Also, he had suddenly remembered that he really didn't know at all where Charles intended to go. That man seemed to be something of a vagabond who would hardly turn down a trip to Alberta if his journey didn't otherwise have a definite goal. On an old map at the Chinaman's Rasmus began to study Alberta's geography. The land of course looked very pretty on paper. When it came down to it, perhaps Paradise was right there.

After Charles came back Rasmus talked with him about the Danish colonists and proposed that he accompany them westward.

Charles not only agreed immediately, but came out with the surprising information that he had owned a homestead there for a long time and farmed near Beaver Coulee. He had been out on long trips to deal in horses. Those that ran away from him down by the Souris River were the remnants of a stud which he had driven east and sold there. Rasmus didn't question him as to why he hadn't gone straight home. It was probably just because there had been some difficulties with his wife, he reasoned. And besides it was certainly not easy to figure out what such a half-breed could hit on. Because Rasmus liked him considerably, he didn't dwell on his motives.

A few hours later the caravan started up and went in a northwesterly direction toward the Saskatchewan River. After the first few days Rasmus and Charles forced Pedersen to rebuild the wagon and get himself a proper team of horses. Pedersen turned over the coins many times before he could bring himself to spend them and tried as well to get the other two to contribute a bit. Since this didn't work, he gave in so as not to lose his retinue.

4.

At a train station farther west the caravan picked up a Dane in his fifties who, being suddenly seized by wanderlust, had taken a trip up from the States. He didn't much resemble an adventurer in other respects. He was a wandering monument of human moroseness; his small surly eyes searched for faults, and his mouth was crooked from mourning over mankind.

"I bet we'll find out he's a holy man," mumbled Rasmus without addressing the words to anyone in particular. "There's no mistaking that mug. It won't be long before he tells me where I'm going to end up."

But Rasmus was completely wrong. Jensen wasn't holy. He was a *freethinker*, and an honest to goodness one at that. It didn't take an hour before they were inaugurated into his views on baptism, communion, confirmation, and burial with clerical participation. "Rubbish," said Jensen. "No God exists, that's clear as day."

"He would have a bad time taking responsibility for you," said Rasmus. "So it's very fortunate for him that he doesn't exist."

Old Pedersen laughed heartily. It amused him to hear someone else being teased for whatever reason. But Jensen went crazy. This was nothing to joke about; it was the most important of all the questions concerning existence. If you didn't find the truth in it, it would be so much the worse for you!

"I don't give much for your faith if you're supposed to go to some kind of hell when you don't even have one. Then of course you only have to choose between two kinds of Hell. You are a big, confounded fool," said Rasmus.

After that round of theology they let religion rest for a while. It wasn't long before they got tired of Jensen. Even in this little wandering society he found the opportunity to spread gossip, and when they were sitting by the fire in the evenings, Rasmus could be seized by an urge to get up, go over and break his vile cabbage stalk neck. But whenever the man sensed danger a lustre came over his expression like a four-year-old child's; he began to look like a dachsund

17

sitting pretty. Then no one had the heart to lay a finger on little Erik Jensen.

- - -

They continually acquired more things to look after. Rasmus had purchased a bulky cage of poultry, and Charles had bought himself eight oxen. Pedersen had the habit of gathering up all kinds of old junk which had been lost or thrown away by people going through the country. Rasmus teased the old fellow by secretly letting his piles of rusted fencing wire, broken wheels and other flotsam fall off the wagon. Sometimes Pedersen would furiously stop the procession while he gathered up his rubbish. "You never know what you might have use for when you're out in the wilds like this! Good wire and almost whole wagon wheels shouldn't just go floating about on the prairie. Who knows, perhaps there are high prices for old iron in Alberta."

None of his sons got mixed up in the quarrels, but the youngest, Frederik, came to hate Rasmus because he didn't bow to his wise father. The eldest kept himself almost always beside Charles, slightly removed from the procession. Little Jensen walked alone thinking that these people didn't know what was best for them.

— — -

It was high summer now. The prairie vegetation in places was a jungle - tall, bristly grass woven together with twining plants and prairie roses into an impenetrable tangle. Around the countless sloughs and marshes stood groups of young trees, deformed and singed stalks like collections of large scouring brushes. They were all rootsuckers which had survived the passing of fire over the prairie. Very rarely a stunted spruce tree could be seen by a swamp; otherwise for the most part it was willow and scrub poplar. In the marshes lived swarms of waterfowl, and butterflies hovered like golden leaves over the parched land. Each day Charles went after game; he often caught it without a gun, however he might manage that. Light-brown gophers peeped curiously at the procession; their mouths twitched, and they threw up their tails - zip, headfirst into their holes and then up again to watch the excitement going on. In the lakes the muskrat appeared like a bit of floating wood, slowly swimming in safety; its intelligent little eye shone in the angle of its wake. In the waterholes stood its mounds of grass and twigs; it was prepared for winter, seeing to it that the breathing holes were in order. At sunset thousands of blackbirds gathered out on the rush-clad islets of the marshes. Whenever Charles shot his gun out there, the blackbird flocks rose up like a cloud of smoke from an explosion.

After the sun had set coyote began to challenge the night, first with a couple of notes as from a cracked bell, then with a prolonged howling which came from everywhere and nowhere. After the first yelp the half-wild dog which followed the convoy, and which Rasmus had named Nicoline, began to dance restlessly, and when the coyote became silent, Nicoline began to bellow - like neither a dog nor a coyote; she had a voice like a woman giving birth.

Pedersen would grin and pull his beard. "We certainly have music with us! We can't complain!"

But Jensen looked reproachfully at him and maintained that Nicoline had an ungodly voice. Charles should shoot her rather than the coyotes, the skins of which he plastered all over the wagon so that it stank to high heaven.

Rasmus answered that since Jensen was a freethinker, it wasn't his business whether Nicoline's howl was ungodly or not. And if the smell of coyote skins did not suit his ugly nose, he could just clear out. Had anyone sent for him perhaps?

Then Jensen became sweet-tempered again. Ha, ha, Rasmus was so witty. But he was glowering. Someday he'd get a chance to get back at this big-talking fellow. And so he controlled himself. He was just as faithful and spiteful as Nicoline. A person got food, of course. Yes, indeed, he did his bit too, that was for sure; these people wouldn't be fit for very much if he weren't along. Actually everything depended on him. He moved his hand to his breast pocket, as he had a habit of doing, and continued his litany of self-pity - "No, it isn't easy in this world when you're a poor man."

Rasmus tramped over to him. "'Water to blood and a multitude of frogs and flies afterward plagued Egypt,'" he quoted. "You can't get water here; that down there is salt. And the little girls' eyes are completely swollen shut from mosquito bites. Listen, Jensen, you must have forgotten to pass around the wagon grease. What are you trotting around with it for? Give it here. I want to smear those mosquito bites. Charles, you'd better saddle up again and find water with that delicate nose of yours."

Charles rode after water. Jensen was sullen. "As you command," he said.

Rasmus turned around quickly. "You're a damned nuisance, Jensen. You either hold us up with that bad leg of yours or some other nonsense. You're a mangy freethinker. You can just keep your trap shut. What a jerk! Going around here complaining and getting good food. Gather wood? No thanks! Make a fire? No thanks! Skin a coyote? No thanks! Cook food? No thanks! But boy, can Jensen eat and make trouble!" Rasmus indignantly put a handful of wagon grease on the head of one of the girls, but he made her laugh anyway. Then he put a rabbit on a spit and started rotating it seriously while he treated Theodor and Frederik to a story about an unpleasant person down in Montana who always lived at other peoples' expense. He had the world's surliest face, especially when someone had made him gather wood against his will, said Rasmus, as Jensen came with an armload of branches in order silently to buy absolution. "But there's this thing about wood," Rasmus lectured on, "It just sputters and smokes and doesn't give off a bit of warmth if the fire isn't built with love. Love! Do you think Jensen there has any of that? Phooey!"

"Ingratitude is the way of the world," said Jensen bitterly, and made no further trip to gather wood.

"In a little while you'll see Jensen eat. Bless me how he can eat. And gulp down those bottles Charles is bringing. Isn't that right, Jensen?"

And Rasmus kept on. But Jensen reacted like Nicoline. She stole, and when she got a board thrown at her, she wagged her tail or flew into a rage, whatever the seriousness of the assault called for. As long as it was a joke she showed her teeth, but if it got serious she crept on her belly and wagged her tail. "Bad blood," said Charles whenever he saw that, but his words in some mystical way seemed to refer to Jensen more than to Nicoline. Neither was easy to get rid of once one had latched on to you. The dog of course could be shot if it didn't behave, and Jensen of course took some of the mosquito bites. You didn't let him live just for the sake of beauty, Rasmus had once said. Jensen couldn't forgive him for that. Even though he hadn't been in the habit of noticing when mosquitoes bit him, after that day he couldn't endure them. He felt the mosquitoes hovering about his ears like Rasmus's maliciously subtle contempt. For some time he loathed them far more than he did Rasmus.

- - -

Charles was strangely restless when he came back with the full water bottles. He didn't seem to be listening to the talk of the camp, and in the middle of a rash story about St. Peter and a freethinker, Rasmus suddenly became serious, grew silent and strolled over to Charles.

"What is it?"

"I don't know," said Charles, "but something's going to happen tonight."

"What's going to happen?"

Charles shook his head. "Who knows. But the gophers are whining, and the hawks aren't swooping. The coyotes have stopped howling."

"Well...what..." mumbled Rasmus. "Of course sometimes they're silent. Do you think there's a prairie fire coming?"

Their eyes met.

"Yes," said Charles.

Rasmus looked over at the wagon where the little girls were chattering, and he made a frightened movement.

"God help us, Charles. And we have both children and animals. It's no good running, either, because we don't know what direction -"

"No, we have to stay. Maybe we'll manage. There's water here, of course -But the animals - it's worse for them."

A couple of deep wrinkles had come over Rasmus's face.

"We'll drive the wagon out into the slough," he said, "pack it full of wet grass and tie the animals to it. The chickens and the children can be inside it, and the rest of us can balance on the sides, I guess."

Charles walked up a hill.

"Nothing to see," he said shaking his head, "but look at the horses now. We'll soon have to get them tied."

The horses were dancing and threw their heads up, sniffing the air. Rasmus caught them and tied them with the oxen beside the wagon.

Pedersen and Jensen looked at him in surprise. They were just thinking of going to bed for the night.

"What's the meaning of this?" asked Jensen.

"Oh," said Rasmus lightly, "it's just the devil who's loose because we're trailing around with a freethinker."

Jensen didn't ask again. Pedersen had become uneasy; he stood up on the wagon and looked around. "I don't see anything," he said.

Rasmus took no time for long explanations. He began to hitch the horses to the wagon.

"Fire's coming before long. We have to get the wagon into the water. Pedersen, Jensen, Theodor and Frederik - start picking grass like you've never done before in your miserable lives. Throw it into the wagon. Chuck everything in the slough that can't get lost and that won't get hurt by water."

None of them was especially willing. They thought the whole thing was nonsense; who could see or smell any fire?

The moon rose, red as the sun going down in a summer evening's haze, four times as large. The coyotes began to yelp here and there, but immediately became silent again. Rasmus noted it. Fire or no fire - *something* was going to happen, whatever it might be...

He stopped the wagon by the edge of the slough until something tangible should appear.

A little later Charles came. "The fire is coming from the west. It's filling the whole horizon from north to south. We couldn't ride away from it on the best horses in Canada."

The horses didn't want to go into the water, nor the oxen either; they tore and pulled at their harnesses, each on its own side. While Rasmus directed the

21

team, Charles drove the others on with his leather whip. The children screamed, the poultry cackled, the oxen bellowed madly while Rasmus swore a blue streak.

A mountain of darkness grew in the west, extinguishing the stars. Coyotes went past, standing for a moment half on their tails with forelegs in the ground and tongues flaring out between dagger-like teeth. Rabbits were running in all directions both toward the fire and away from it. A weasel rushed past like a writhing serpent, and gophers ran into the water to get it over with at once. The skunk plodded off, crying with every part of its body, and the badger splashed next to the bank snarling; it didn't want to go any further; it sat down on its tail in the mud and bared its teeth toward what was coming. All the prairie animals went past, silent and panting, a horde struck by madness, the coyote side by side with the rabbit, owls and hawks in the middle of flocks of peaceful birds.

The wagon now stood well away from the shore, and the men poured water up onto the grass, placing the children under a blanket soaked in water. The animals now stood silent by the sides of the wagon, pricking up their ears, their legs firmly stuck in the mud. Whenever they lifted one leg, the others became even more firmly stuck. It tired them out. Each man stood down in the water on the spokes of the wheels. They soaked their hats with water and filled them with wet grass before they put them back on.

Charles, however, didn't know the meaning of the word "truce". He stood by the bank shooting the coyotes as they came, throwing them into the water to keep the fire from damaging the skins. At last he joined the others, and a minute later the fire was there.

First a hot surge of air, then a rain of fire and heat explosions in the grass - then the world disappeared in smoke and fire. Rasmus stepped down into the mud and began to throw water in over the wagon with a bucket. Charles portioned out the wet grass in small clumps on to the heads of the animals.

The heat rose. The two boys leaned back from the wheelspokes so that only their eyes and noses stuck up over the surface of the water. The little girls cried heart-rendingly in the wagon, and Rasmus sobbed along with them while he threw water in over them and the half dead chickens. He heaved a bucket full of the muddy water over his own head, then kept on, threw a bucket into the face of Pedersen, whose beard was on the point of being singed, chucked the next one over the head of Jensen, who was praying pitifully to the Almighty. You're a spirited freethinker it seems to me, Rasmus thought, and gave him one more bucketful. "Stop your howling," he screamed. "Do you think the Almighty will help us if he hears you're here? Shut your mouth!"

And he began to throw water over Charles, who was on the way up into the wagon to look after the children.

"Stop!" shouted Charles. "Have you forgotten that the wagon is water-tight? The children's heads are above water, but I won't vouch for your chickens. We don't need any more water."

He sat down in the bottom of the wagon to comfort the children, while Rasmus found an outlet for his energy by first throwing a couple of more buckets of water at Jensen's head and then splashing around after the dead coyotes and fastening them to the wagon. The moon's light was smothered in the thick smoke. The heat was frightful. But down near the surface of the water it was possible to bear it; there was a little space between the water and the smoke which hung over the slough like a ceiling. Rasmus became quiet. The danger was past. In an hour the smoke would lift, though only God knew what misfortunes had happened on the prairie that night.

Pedersen hadn't said very much. Jensen was also silent now; he didn't have any more use for the Almighty. Only Charles's quiet voice was heard from the wagon where he was telling the girls that soon now the whole thing would be over - a fire like that just came to chase away all the mosquitoes which were biting so badly. Tomorrow they'd just see, there wouldn't be any mosquitoes at all.

The oxen chewed their cud in the middle of the destruction of the world. In on land crackling sounds came from the earth, and now and then there were real explosions with earth being slung into the air or stones bursting. The ground still smouldered, but the bright fire was several miles off, a wall of flame going over the land from the west to the east.

- - -

"Are the girls cold?" Rasmus came over to ask.

Theodor coughed a bit.

"I think it's more likely they're cooked," he answered hoarsely. "Heavens, what a country! Burned off from one end to the other in one night."

"Some day it'll be different," said Rasmus. "We'll see to that with the plow. If only the smoke would lift now..."

He tossed his head back and remained standing with his mouth open. Something had struck him hard on the top of his head; objects came roaring down onto the wagon, and one of the girls cried out in pain. Around them the water was splashing as if the slough were suddenly bombarded by bricks. Before anyone could stop to think, a cyclone howled across them.

"Up into the wagon and cover the children!" screamed Charles.

"Oh, God in heaven above, stammered Jensen, "what are you going to let happen now? Am I like the prophet Jonas.?" Something hard banged into his face, and blood spurted from his nose.

Everyone screamed at once in the storm and the choking smoke. Glowing ashes and gravel swept over them; entire bright bonfires came rushing like comets.

"Hail storm!" bellowed Charles. "Up and cover the children!"

But Jensen preferred sticking his head in under the bottom of the wagon while the others protected the wailing children with their bodies. Flashes of lightning rose up from the prairie like glowing branches stretching out under the sky. The thunder rumbled loose, as if the earth were being rent to its core. They were pummeled by chunks of ice; as Rasmus swore, when he once caught his breath, that this was worse than being thrashed by the police in Minneapolis. "And to top it off I hadn't done anything," he screamed to drown out the storm, the thunder and the falling ice. "Not a thing! But a hail of blows is just as hard to take, even if you're innocent, I can bear witness to that. They pounded my neck and back, my arms and rear end as I ran, and when I fell, I had my other side up, so they made that black and blue too..."

And Rasmus in a shrill voice kept on describing what the police had done to him in Minneapolis as the hail crashed down and the prairie lay like an oven with lightning twisting on the ground and lightning climbing into the sky. Three times he was on the point of telling how much compensation he got, but each time the thunder broke loose like a collision of worlds.

Down under the wagon Jensen had gotten as far as the "Prayer When One Is in a Storm and Great Peril on the Sea". "Preserve us, our ship and cargo as you preserved your servant Noah in the days of the flood, and take care that what I have in my wallet will not be splashed to nothing now that I have worked and saved for so long. I have never harmed a fly. You know I have always..."

What Jensen had always done the Almighty didn't find out. Water, hail, grass, bird coop, children and four grownups were more than the wagon could hold. The bottom fell out of it unexpectedly. Jensen was the first to disappear in the mud, and he was the last to be found. Charles came up with a child in each hand. The children were completely apathetic. They could neither be terrified nor consoled any longer. Charles stood for a moment without seeing the others. Then something grabbed his leg, and he kicked it away angrily. "What's the big idea?" Then came Theodor; he was coughing a great deal. "The children?" he said with difficulty. "I was looking for them in the mud."

The next one was Frederik. "Thank God you've got them," he said, relieved. Then Charles understood, and when someone again took hold of his leg, there was a swing in his kick. Old Pedersen appeared momentarily. "Oh, thank God they're all right," he groaned. A couple of legs appeared above the surface. They belonged to Rasmus, who was still searching with his hands. Eventually he too surfaced. "Oh, *you* found them. I should have known," he said crossly. "I've eaten several pounds of tadpoles. Where are the chickens and Jensen? Oh, that's right, up with you onto the sides of the wagon. *Of course, he was under the bottom of the wagon,* and we're standing on it!"

They climbed up while Rasmus twisted around like an otter and disappeared. Not many seconds passed before he came back with Jensen, whom he hanged up over the edge of the wagon with his head down on the inner side and his legs outside. Rasmus looked helplessly at the others. What were they going to do?

Frederik saw that since a lot of water was running out of Jensen's mouth the matter would probably take care of itself. They consoled themselves for the time being with that, and Rasmus swam out to his bird coop which was sailing around at the mercy of the wind and waves. There was no hail any more, but waterfalls of tepid rain were streaming down. The thunder grew distant, and the first signs of day asserted themselves. They talked about it in surprised tones. No one could believe such a long time had passed.

Jensen came around and began to sob loudly. The girls were sleeping soaked through and through on Charles's chest. Rasmus struck Jensen on the top of his head, but he just cried all the more, and so Rasmus let him carry on.

5.

It was a glorious morning. The sun glimmered in the black wet porridge of prairie. For miles it lay as if strewn with jewels. By the edges of the slough they gathered charcoal and made a bonfire to dry their clothes and prepare food. The children slept soundly in the warm mire. One horse was dead, probably from fright. Nicoline, whom everyone had forgotten - she hadn't been seen since the previous evening - appeared with singed fur and a tail shortened by several inches. She peered around brazenly, as she usually did, and now was nasty enough to be shot, Rasmus thought. But in that case, of course, Jensen should really be done away with since he was no longer necessary as a diverter of mosquitoes - so it was probably best to let Nicoline live.

Rasmus began nursing his poultry by the fire. Life came into the rooster and seven chickens. They could still form the basis of a flock. He fried one of the dead ones for breakfast.

There was a lot to do before they could go on. Pedersen and his sons were in the process of repairing the wagon. Charles was skinning his coyotes, while Nicoline looked on, gloating maliciously. Jensen had gone out for a morning walk.

While Rasmus was turning his clothes which were hanging out to dry, he spied something alive on the top of one of the scorched prairie hills. It disappeared almost immediately. Rasmus speculated about what it could be but pretended not to notice. A little later it showed itself again. In spite of the great distance Rasmus was certain it was Jensen's head which was popping up and turning watchfully toward the camp. What was going on? With a glance out of the corner of his eye Rasmus worked on. Soon Jensen's head was there again. Rasmus began to ruminate. This reminded him a little too much of a coyote lying in wait. He put down his pipe, tightened his belt and got ready. The next time Jensen's head went cautiously down, Rasmus was off, and he reached the top of the hill just as Jensen had almost got up to take another look. The man became deathly pale under the dirt on his face; his lower jaw sank.

"Nice weather", Rasmus said.

Words failed Jensen. He made an attempt at movement with both arms and legs but did nothing.

"I suppose you're looking to see if we're doing anything, huh?" said Rasmus. "Up to something we mustn't see, mister? Afraid of somebody coming to outrage your decency, sir? No funny business with us, old boy! I tell you. Did you snitch something last night? Shut up! I know you're stealing. And you're only still with us because you're an old hobbler. What are you doing here? Why were you scared?"

Rasmus's eyes searched over the surroundings. Down at the foot of the hill the ashes had been scraped away, exposing several light patches.

"What's that down there?" asked Rasmus sharply.

Jensen suddenly acted like a cornered rat. Curses flooded out of his mouth. Whose business was it? Did he answer to anyone? What did a puppy like that think? Wasn't the prairie big enough for all of them? Go to hell!

Little Jensen had no idea of how close he was to getting his neck broken, for Rasmus had caught him pilfering several times and now thought that Jensen had been looting in the night's confusion. He took hold of himself, though, and began walking down the hill. Jensen jumped on him. Rasmus's amazement was so great that it alone nearly toppled him. His arms started moving for a couple of seconds, and Jensen disappeared into a pile of ashes. There was a nice hole, round as a circle, where he disappeared. He quickly came out on the opposite side of the heap, crying, crawling on all fours. "Again and again!" he wailed. "Again and again I'm pursued and tormented; that's the way it was when I was a child right up until I was confirmed, and it's been exactly the same since. Wickedness and blasphemy have tormented me and taken the light out of my life. What the devil business is it of yours what I do? Can't an old man be allowed to do what he wants? Last March I was fifty, the seventh of March, but bad luck will pursue me until the last days of my life."

Rasmus looked at him impressed. Truly that man had a mastery of words! But he still wanted to study the situation down there.

Jensen followed after him complaining. Rasmus· opened his eyes wide: Banknotes, large and small, lay nicely smoothed out on the ground to dry in the sun. There was a fortune, several thousand good dollars.

"Well, you can't have stolen all of this here. But now I'll tell you something in all friendliness. You have stayed with us because you pretended to be poor. I've known all along that you're a bum. But now it turns out you're rich. We've had enough of you. I hope we hit a train station pretty soon so we can get rid of you."

Infuriated, Rasmus went back to the camp. He didn't mention Jensen's money. For who could know - Pedersen also loved money.

Rasmus Dansker had been born with very few illusions about people.

- - -

Toward daybreak Jensen came to ask for mercy. It wasn't easy being old. He was supporting a family in Denmark who were waiting for him to save enough money for a little farm in the old country...

Rasmus didn't believe a word of it. But he always felt sorry for people who lied. He didn't speak seriously any more about driving Jensen off.

Strange signs and mirages appeared that day and night over the hot prairie where the steam rose from the ashes. In the air a sea with distant sails was reflected; the image faded, and another one followed with ice and snow, enormous chunks of ice and cold deserted plains. It was replaced in turn by farms, blissful green fields, gardens where trees stood, their boughs laden with fruit.

The birds were returning already; the prairie lark sat in the ashes and poured out its troubles: its chicks hadn't escaped. The prairie chickens came in noisy flocks; the laughing sound of their wings made the land alive: hi, hi, hi! ha, ha, ha! A coyote full of life and "I made it" roamed about looking for nice roast meat. A gopher came to life out in the marsh when the sun had dried its pelt; it moved a little, but a hawk saw it and made off with it...

The sun went down over the burned plains, blood red. It was as though its uppermost edge couldn't quite keep up but was caught in red and lilac bands of colour which finally burst. Then the whole sun went through a strange rebirth, hung suddenly with its full form over the edge of the sky again until it faded and disappeared without setting. But where it had been, a human skull came into shape from the haze and rested its chin on the horizon, its unfathomable gaze lying over the darkening plain where the black hills began to breathe, breasts rising and falling over the heart of the world.

- - -

They slept deeply that night. However, the whole camp was awakened in the night by some shrill whistling. Everyone sat up and stared at Jensen, for the sound was coming from him. With his knees bent and completely naked he was jumping straight up and down out in the ashes. His whistling was undoubtedly intended to be monotone, but the jumps made his belly shake. When he had whistled himself tired he continued jumping and began to howl worse than any coyote. Nicoline put her tail between her legs and disappeared.

"Damned if he's not walking in his sleep," whispered Pedersen.

"*Walking,*" sneered Rasmus. "Can't you see he's jumping?"

Jensen suddenly straightened up and looked around in confusion.

"Are you finished now?" asked Rasmus. "Very nice performance. Where do you learn something like that?"

"It's an illness I have," mumbled Jensen and turned his back.

Rasmus lay down laughing.

"Look, something like that comes from being a freethinker, little Jensen. It's a good thing we won't be dragging you along with us into heaven!"

- - -

One day in pouring rain the caravan reached a ranch in the neighbourhood of Youngstown just inside Alberta. They stopped - partly because the rain made it difficult to make any headway, but also to salvage their provisions and make repairs.

A middle-aged couple lived there. The houses were primitive, with holes and cracks everywhere. Inside were two rooms, one for women and one for men. The rain kept on pouring down; the water stood on the prairie in clear lakes. Chickens and pigs walked around soaked and numb in the mire. It was wet and dark, both outside and in; the air like cloudy glass. In the stall Rasmus and Charles worked at the grindstone while the owner sat with a sagacious air in an empty manger calculating his annual accounts with chalk on the backside of a shovel blade. He alternately sighed and grunted approvingly. Eventually with two fingers he collected the plug of tobacco out of his mouth and threw it over to a pig which ate it with relish, craftily moving its white eyebrows up and down. The man bowed his head, placed his elbows on his knees and tore at his hair. The rain drummed monotonously onto the domed roof of the stall. Charles tested the edge of his knife on his thumbnail while Rasmus moodily continued turning the stone in order to avoid the inconvenience of starting it up again. He was sort of thinking. Actually he was seeing visions. Holy Madonna, what a girl over there in the house! It would be good to have her close by on rainy days. Could she be the daughter of that old blusterer over there? There couldn't be a worse father-in-law. Better to stay here and wait and see - and let that silly procession move on without him.

Of course you could tie your scarf around her mouth and take her along. Charles was a peach of a fellow. He only took offense when someone stepped on his toes on purpose. Everything else he left up to people themselves. But in

29

addition to him of course there were the two old fellows - though Pedersen, surely he'd be only too pleased if a girl came along who could fuss over his children. Jensen could have a sock in the kisser.

After that study in social psychology Rasmus sighed deeply. Of course there was the catch that he couldn't bring himself to treat such a lovely girl that way, even if the desire and will were there. Ha! Jensen would have begun at once to lay himself out to please...

They came back over into the house, and Rasmus looked intently at the girl as she was kneading dough. It was hot there in the room, and the door stood open out to the rain. A pig or hen ventured just a bit inside the door but was scared away by Eva's shout.

Eva! Strange he hadn't thought before about how pretty that name actually was. It became more than a designation, became something which could be touched, acquiring dimension and form - Eva!

Pedersen came in and informed them that an itinerant doctor was approaching with his wagon. Pedersen was enjoying himself. What a horse!

Rasmus peeked out the window. There came the wagon. The horse was a lean, unshod nag. The vehicle sank up to its axles in the road, but it didn't occur to the doctor to get off; he was sitting raised up high above the whole world on the roof of the closed wagon saying, "Gee up!" Now and then without any warning he exploded into a shower of curses and whip lashes, each time causing the horse to stand still until he was finished. When he lowered the whip and became silent, the skeleton horse weighed the situation for a while before it went on again. "Well, that certainly helped," shouted the man of science triumphantly.

When he came to the middle of the farmyard he stopped and looked around probingly. Nobody bothered to come out. Remaining seated for a bit, the doctor cast a sidelong glance at the house, but since an invitation still was not forthcoming he let go of the reins, climbed down and went to the door. He waited, then coughed in preparation and went in. He said hello, got a hello back and looked fixedly at each person in the room. Then he took off his raincoat and hung it on a nail.

"Wet today," said the man of the house.

"Beastly wet today," confirmed the doctor.

With that the conversation stopped momentarily while the doctor rolled a cigarette and stared searchingly at each and every person in the room.

"Anybody sick here?"

"No, esteemed sir."

The doctor lit the cigarette and addressed the farmer in a serious tone:

"Still I can tell you for sure that your daughter has anemia."

"No, she doesn't."

"You shouldn't say that," came the answer. "It's clear enough."

"No it isn't."

"How do you know that your daughter doesn't have anemia?"

"I don't have any daughter."

The doctor remained unperturbed.

"Perhaps this young lady is not your daughter, but she has anemia."

"No I haven't," answered the aforesaid lady. "You're not going to make me believe something's wrong with me. I'm not as stupid as that Mrs. Hughes who you said had gallstones!"

"Mrs. Hughes *had* gallstones, and I cured her," the doctor said emphatically.

He suddenly turned around toward Rasmus.

"You're looking poorly, mister."

"Oh," said the master of the house peevishly, "that man is on the point of dying."

"I can see that," said the doctor.

"That is, from laughing."

Those present uttered a howl of laughter. The doctor went over to the stove and warmed his hands.

"Everybody has something secretly wrong with him," he said composedly, "which sooner or later will cause difficulties if an experienced man doesn't take care of it in time. This young lady's anemia perhaps doesn't inconvenience her now. But in four or five years it could be her death if it isn't cured soon. In ten years it *will* be her death. Because anemia comes from a lack of veins in the blood."

He lifted a finger pontificatingly:

"The veins are the moving ones, the arteries are fixed. When there aren't enough veins then the arteries can't flow, but rather fill up the veins until you die of a heart attack without any warning. Like a thief in the night!"

The passage from the Scriptures made an impression on the host.

"It's really bad," he said and looked searchingly at the girl, as if he expected her to topple over at any moment - like a thief in the night. But the girl didn't let herself be upset.

"My blood is flowing quickly enough. I cut my finger yesterday and it downright squirted out. A little anemia wouldn't have been amiss then."

"May I see that finger? Look after that sort of thing! Out here where there are so many water holes, germs thrive in the air, and an open sore is a dangerous thing both for you and those you prepare food for. Come here..."

"Go away," she answered.

"You should bear in mind..."

"Do you want a wash rag in your face?"

The medicineman sat down distressed. While he continued deploring the health of those present, Rasmus stood by the window studying his wagon, which was painted with advertisements and accounts of miraculous cures. There were solemn exhortations concerning the stomach, eyes, corns, nervousness and bad breath which bespoke internal defects and turned the heart of a beloved one cold. Rasmus went out and peeked into the wagon. It was full of strange things and reeked of sulphur.

The doctor left the ranch after having contributed to its provisions with a bottle of American oil and ten pounds of axle grease.

Rasmus looked out of the corner of his eye at Eva. There was a woman to have on a farm; there was good stuff in her. It was usually the easiest thing in the world to make women believe they had all sorts of illnesses, especially when there were strange and interesting cases of veins and arteries. But no, Eva didn't go for that kind of newfangled rubbish; she was first rate through and through. It seemed also as though she knew it. A little ignorance on that point could probably have made the whole thing easier.

Alas, it was so easy to deal with men. If you wanted something of them, then you said so. If there were something wrong so words didn't suffice, you let your fists do the talking. As far as he was concerned men could do what they wanted to as long as they didn't get in his way. You didn't always want to give women that right. But in return you couldn't say that to them. Rasmus was paralysed whenever Eva laughed at him; his movements became clumsy and affected. The woman was a very great puzzle.

The next morning the sun was shining, but Rasmus pretended it had never been his intention to travel on so quickly. First purchases had to be made - a potato harvest could probably still be gathered in.

The day after that Rasmus found no excuse to stay. But it was so hopeless to have to leave Eva to all those cowboys going to and fro on the ranch! Almost every sentence he uttered ended most artificially in a remark about his coming back on a trip at springtime, while he looked everywhere but into Eva's eyes. Gradually she became silent and began to look at him sidelong while she tended to her work.

"So we'll see each other in the spring," she said when he gave her his hand in parting.

"Yes," he said thankfully. And he was happy as never before when he let the whip whistle and the horses set themselves in motion. Jensen on the contrary was more sullen than anyone hitherto had seen him. He had got a boxing on the ears - and on an empty stomach to boot.

With Nicoline prowling in circles around the caravan, they headed on west.

6.

Rasmus reined in his horse high on a hill and scanned the land. They were on their way through tracts of forest that included large lakes. After looking about for a bit he rode back to the others.

"Can you figure it out?" he asked. "This land isn't the way it ought to be..."

Pedersen looked at the wagon wheels which cut deeply into the ground. They noticed their wet footsteps as they walked.

"I don't like it," he said. "We have come to a poor land."

Charles calmed them.

"It won't last very long. Places like this can be found all over the prairie."

"There's nothing alive anywhere in sight," said Rasmus. "That bothers me most. Not a fly, no rabbits, not a bird. It's so quiet here that there's a ringing in my ears..."

"Yes," said Charles. "It's the land of death. No one can say why. Four times I've come through it, but I've never seen any life. The bottom is bogland - you can break up whole chunks of it - but it's dry. You can dig and dig but not come to anything except loose turf and branches."

"There could still be animals here," said Rasmus. "Why isn't there even a miserable mouse? I don't understand it."

Charles shook his head.

"No one understands why. There are evil spirits here, I think. Plants and trees can grow, but animals can't live. They die of grief...and I can tell you that we have a twenty hour journey to fresh water. The water in these lakes is as salty as the Pacific."

"Then I'd think that's explanation enough..."

"No, for it rains here just as much as anywhere else. As far as the water's concerned, animals could certainly survive. There are brooks with water here that horses like but that humans get sick from. All the animals like to drink it."

Rasmus stood silent a while and looked about. The sky wasn't as it should have been either; it hung so rusty over the forests. Suddenly he was gripped

33

with a burning thirst. Was it because Charles had been talking about salt water? But then a vision of what he thirsted for spread out before his eyes.

The sea.

It came over him like an unbearable pain that it was hundreds of miles away, an interminable trip. He was seized by a desire to take this land with him and spread it out on the coasts of Maine so these miserable trees and the poor steppe would droop down toward the dash of the waves of the Atlantic.

The caravan moved on. Without anyone's noticing, Charles, who rode forward, changed direction to the southwest. At a clearing overgrown with tall grass he came to a stop. The others caught up with him and looked in surprise at a granite boulder which rose up over the grass. There was an inscription on it, executed in awkward letters:

Gertrude Wilkinson.

Walter Wilkinson.

Dora Wilkinson.

Peace, Perfect Peace.

"It's a gravestone," whispered Theodor.

"Yes, it is," said Charles. "They say that once you could have drunk the water here. Then an English family came and settled. There were three children. One by one they laid them here. It's the land of death."

Rasmus looked about and shuddered. Here the children were buried while year by year the wilderness won back the farm. Now only one large gray stone with the chiseled words Peace, Perfect Peace, rose up on the parched hill where the winds wailed.

So much appeared in his mind. He saw the broken man kneeling, labouriously carving the names of the dead children in the stone while in the land of death it was completely quiet. And suddenly something rose to the forefront of Rasmus's consciousness: he saw his own mother by a fresh grave in South Dakota. It concealed his brother, her son...and then a jump forward in time: The withered flowers on the mound of earth over her own coffin, a few paces from the old grave.

Peace, Perfect Peace...

He felt again a searing thirst, and remembered that this was the second time in his life the longing for a coast and waves billowing toward it had come over him like a torment. The first time had been in Denmark when he went to serve as a shepherd boy. He had come up onto a hill that first evening without knowing what he was after. At the top, where he saw a landscape like the one he had left with hill curving into hill, a disappointment and sense of homelessness gripped him, and he went back crying. The fjord was gone.

Panic had struck him, and he felt like a caged bird.

He closed his eyes and sought security by whispering a series of names to himself. The Pacific, Saskatchewan River, Hudson Bay, Lake Manitoba, The Atlantic. But it was as though there were no deliverance from these miles and miles of land...

Again he opened his eyes and looked at the stone. Those children had come from a land by the sea. Now they lay down there listening to the waves.

Peace, Perfect Peace.

- - -

They stood with bowed heads around the stone, each one far off in his own thoughts. Charles's glance secretly slid over them. For a second there was something resembling triumph in his eyes.

"Let's get going," said Rasmus.

And again they continued west, as Nicoline bickered with the coyotes.

- - -

Once more they came to smiling regions. Pedersen began appraising the land; at last he was in the kingdom of his dreams. He didn't know himself what power it was that had driven him to Alberta. Coincidence, probably - he had thought about Canada only in general terms until he got to Montreal. There one day he had seen a fairly forbidding store, the show window of which was designed to send a cold shiver down one's backbone. It was an awful display of wax and printed matter - don't hesitate, enquire within, you won't be cured so cheaply anywhere else. The whole thing was mostly reminiscent of a mixture of third-class entertainment and barbershop. Behind a bit of glass in the door a muderous eye had watched his movements. In a rotten mood he went away - he wanted to get far away from Montreal. Being prepared in this manner, fate saw to it that he next spied a coloured placard with abundant fruits and glossy cattle. Go to sunny Alberta!

Pedersen devoured the picture with his eyes and thought about the store he had just seen. A week later he was on his way west toward paradise in Alberta. A hundred times he could have taken a profitable homestead along the way. But there was nothing to be done about that. It had to be Alberta.

Westward they went. Day after day, week after week. It was in the middle of the glowing height of summer that the journey ended toward evening as naturally as though it had been determined right from Moose Jaw that they were going to camp on this particular spot of earth around the wagon for the last time. They had been moving on for a long time without speaking when

Charles said,

"I live behind those trees to the north over there. And here you have Beaver Coulee. I dare say you'll like living around it."

"What?" said Pedersen vacantly and looked about. Neither he nor any of the others could see what Charles was talking about - and yet, there was a faint shadow far to the north. Probably it was behind that forest that he lived. But the coulee? There was nothing to see but the endless prairie on all sides.

Charles smiled.

"We've been climbing upward for several minutes. Take a couple of steps more."

They did so hesitatingly, and stopped as if paralysed. Under them stretched mile-long intersecting valleys with wooded slopes. In the valleys lay one landscape as if inside the other; in the bottom of the valley were other hills and dales. Some were as if built by intelligent creatures, sugar loafs or raised domes, some flatly cut off at the top. Fences made of bushes ran along the watercourses down there. A moose was slowly making its way from south to north. Charles was after it in a twinkling down through a gully in the enormous valleyside. There was a wealth of flowers, and the heat hung trembling in the crevices.

"It's the Garden of Eden," said Pedersen quietly. "Here's where we'll live. Do you hear, Theodor and Frederik and Else and Mette? It's the Garden of Eden, and we're going to live here!"

The rifle cracked, the moose jumped to the side, still running as it fell. Charles came back.

"A stray," he said. "If none have been shot while I've been east, only two have been taken here in the last thirty years."

"I would have thought there would always be enough of that kind of meat here," Pedersen laughed and pulled his beard. His eyes shone. "We'll put up a house over there on that level clearing. Then we'll have shelter and a view over the whole area - good land all around. Heavens, yes, like a big dance floor. So we finally got here! I guess there's no need to take out a homestead right away? It's just a waste of time."

"It's only three hours' ride to town," said Charles. "So you should do so all the same."

"But a *station*?" asked Rasmus cautiously.

"They figure that the town will be a station in a few years."

Now Pedersen pulled his beard with both hands. "Well, we've really come home, huh Jensen?"

But Jensen's eyes darted here and there; he had now got into that quandary that he had feared for so long. How was he going to establish a partnership with one of them? Which one should it be, and was there a lawyer who could draw up the papers the way he wanted them? Pedersen was surely not so good, he was *stingy*. Rasmus was a fool but could probably be led. He himself was getting on, of course, couldn't be expected to work his fingers to the bone any more. Rasmus? He would be the very one to finance the undertaking, if he could get someone to help. He could be a sort of farmhand and partner. And considering his own worldly experience - that would be good for a young man like Rasmus. Well, actually, if you got right down to it, damned if he didn't feel as if that asshole was practically his own flesh and blood son.

Charles went down to his moose, and Rasmus dug fanatically into the ground with Pedersen's spade. "There will be a dwelling here," he said, sweating. "Good lord, what a dwelling there will be here! Theodor and Frederik, go and cut down some trees. Leave the branches on till you bring them up here. Else and Mette, you girls, you can pick grass, but don't prick your fingers. We need to have grass for the roof of the house and to sleep in. What a bed you'll have! Pick grass, Jensen. Pedersen, fix some food. Damn it, *pick grass, Jensen!* Fix some food, Pedersen."

- - -

But down by the fallen moose stood Charles Villeneuve, the Gaul and the Indian in one person, looking despondently up toward the loud-voiced people, Europeans, who would soon set the plow in his coulee. He himself was a farmer, he himself had shown those people the way. Hadn't his father's family come over from one of those countries and displaced his mother's family from America's soil?... Indeed, Charles had chosen. He wanted to yield to the whites and thin out his blood in the white race. There was no betrayal toward the red men in that, for wasn't he a halfblood who could go to whichever side he wanted? And wasn't it best to lead one's children into that race which would rule? The red man was in many ways superior to the white man, and the conquerors were often well aware of that in the north. Here "injun" was not a term of abuse, and so there was no reason to protest by keeping oneself to the red men - for there wasn't anything out here to protest against. Indeed, Charles had chosen, had become a farmer and wanted to marry a white woman.

But then three years ago he had met a girl here in Beaver Coulee. It was during one of those periods when, naked to the waist, he had hung on the back of his horse for weeks, a lonely Attila, hunting on the prairie. Most certainly, he had chosen! But no one chooses his nature. The Indian and the Gaul had not blended in his mind. Whenever the one lived, the other was dead. And that spring the red man lived and took a girl after his own taste one dark night in Beaver Coulee. Nature had annulled his choice and given him Indian children.

37

Afterward, though, only the Frenchman had lived in Charles Villeneuve.

He looked up over the slopes of the coulee where he knew every tree and every block of granite sticking out. There was something newborn over it, now when he saw it in reality. While he had been wandering about in the east, his memory of it had become a little faded.

He remembered that up there on one of the slopes was a block of granite where the melt water had licked a small hole in the middle. You could squeeze your hand through the opening, and inside there was a slightly larger space. He had often thought about how long it had been since the water had begun its work.

Now when he reached the stone he saw that there had been a landslide. The stone was overturned so that the hole was now on the side. Straw and a little down stuck out from it. Charles approached slowly. In the hole was a brooding sparrow.

He stood in thought. Something happens, but it's as if it has never happened. The water licked down into that hole for countless years. Perhaps the process began before the French sailed up the St. Lawrence. Drop after drop fell so that in due course there could be a sparrow nest. And tirelessly the drops worked again on another side of the stone for a new sparrow nest, and meanwhile sparrow mothers for hundreds of years could flutter out from the nest and quench their thirst at the spring.

Charles bowed his head. Right in *his* own day the miracle had happened, and the sparrow had got its nest. In a thousand years...no, now the water would drip in vain. In only a few hundred years there would probably be a city ravaged by light in Beaver Coulee.

Charles suddenly brushed back his long hair, walked down and started swiftly to skin the moose. He threw a glance now and then up to the others and smiled. They were full of energy. Rasmus's ringing shouts echoed in the valleys, and axes resounded in the coulee's bottom. Rasmus wanted to have a house built for them, and it was going to be done immediately. Charles slowly shook his head and again smiled sadly. Of what use was it to be descended from chieftains and noblemen when you were ten years weighing a matter to the core, finally knowing what the right thing was - when you ended the struggles and considerations of the years by doing the irremediable and wrong thing one dark night in Beaver Coulee? He up there, Ross Dane, didn't let the sun go down over his thoughts - he always did the right thing, though most likely neither he himself nor others were always clear whether he thought or acted first. Sometimes it seemed as if he were quite astounded over what he had just done - then he stood on one leg and had gleaming sunshine in his eyes. In such cases Charles did not doubt that Rasmus was confronted with a delayed reflection of what his actions had just been.

    To him - to Rasmus the Dane, Ross Dane - the future belonged.

7.

From day to day the coulee changed its face. Each day brought un-suspected things, each day was a new summer, each day came to a new land. The valleys stood one morning full of red poppies which opened themselves so passionately toward the glowing sun that they enjoyed only one day of maidenhood. The next day their leaves lay in the grass, plants of lost innocence in piles, while the leafless, pregnant heads saw that they were naked, but were not ashamed. Editor Sol walked thoughtfully over the floor of his office contriving new sensations for the world press. He shone tentatively on Rasmus Dansker, who quite rightly began thinking about a girl at Youngstown but stayed where he was. Then the sun made Beaver Coulee yellow for a day and went on to the next column.

- - -

Rasmus knew all about the inland winter, and he knew that it wasn't too early to think about housing. He persuaded Pedersen to give up every effort to raise any kind of crop that year and instead to buy what was necessary to get through the winter. Dwellings had to be started at once, and Rasmus decided without discussion that Pedersen's should be built first. The girls should have a roof over their heads.

Free logs could be dragged here from Indian Forest, as they had named it, but the horses were too slight for that kind of work. If they were merely content with what they themselves could handle, there wouldn't be enough. There were of course Charles's oxen which they could probably borrow. But they weren't broken in.

Rasmus thought about it for a few minutes, then threw himself on one of the horses and rode over to see Charles. He was preparing skins. Three copper-brown children with stiff black hair and hawk noses on their baby faces

41

clung to him when Rasmus came. Charles didn't invite him in, but somewhat later his wife came out. Rasmus was a little startled. She was a tall, strong injun woman with devilish eyes, though remarkably pretty. She had a set of teeth like a bear's.

Rasmus explained what he had come for. Of course, he could borrow the oxen. But Charles shook his head doubtfully - they were pretty wild animals to be hitched up to a wagon. Charles had still not succeeded in breaking them in. If Rasmus wanted to try, then Charles would be only too pleased. As a matter of fact he could just as well buy four of them.

Rasmus did business at once and took all eight with him. "I'll straighten them out all right," he told him. "And then you'll get yours back when they're willing to pull."

Above the coulee Rasmus made his preparations. The oxen allowed themselves to be hitched up willingly enough.

"Pretty animals, pretty animals," said Pedersen. "It will work out all right."

But Rasmus didn't say anything. He was satisfied to take two in front and tie the others to a tree.

"May I come along?" asked Frederik when Rasmus climbed up into the wagon.

"No," said Rasmus curtly. "Go away. Now! *Get up; get up!*"

The oxen took a step, but when they felt the wagon they were pulling, they stood still. Rasmus swung his whip. The animals didn't move. Then the screeching strap of leather fell. Ten seconds later the vehicle was several hundred meters away.

Rasmus held the reins slack and let the animals go thundering off. He hoped that some gracious fate would keep the wagon clear of larger stones, but the risk of smashing it was something that had to be taken. It wasn't long before he was out of sight. Whenever the wagon leapt over bushes and stones during the perilous run-away ride, Rasmus flew around inside it. A couple of times he didn't land on his feet after having been thrown into the air. He hit his elbows and got the skin scraped off his nose. But when the oxen slowed their speed, the whip fell again, the animals bellowed in a rage and started running. Then they stopped suddenly, wriggled a little in the harness and lay down. Rasmus gave himself just enough time to take a breath, let the whip whine and fall again. The oxen didn't move. He struck again and again with all the strength that was in both of his enormous arms where the muscles lay like ropes - get up! But the beasts didn't move.

Rasmus dried blood and sweat from his eyes. "Well, by God you're stubborn! It's always exactly as Charles says."

By now Rasmus was angry though not confused. His face was diabolically distorted as he pulled a twelve foot chain up out of his voluminous pants pockets and arranged the chain links in the bottom of the wagon. His look was dangerous. "Well, so you don't want to obey Ross Dane! Now you'll get it - and that in the Devil's name!" He started swinging the chain, and swung it four or five times in a circle before it fell on one of the oxen from head to tail. It bellowed and wanted to get up but couldn't because of the other one...then the chain fell again, and the other one got up. Rasmus let the chain go and grasped the reins. Again the wild chase continued; Rasmus was beaten to a pulp, endlessly falling and getting back on his feet.

At sunset he came driving to the coulee with two gentle oxen. He himself, though, looked as if he had been thoroughly beaten for a long time. He continued the next day while all the others went into the forest and felled trees. Those oxen were on the point of costing him both his life and his health. But when ten days had passed he could tell the animals what they had to do. Charles got his four oxen back, and Rasmus began hauling logs to Beaver Coulee.

One day as Rasmus was coming out to the woods with the oxen after a load, Jensen began talking to him.

"I don't think you really see what's going on, little Rasmus..."

"What's going on?"

"Well, think about it. Here comes Pedersen driving along on the prairie and getting people to follow him. They save him and his children and everything he owns while the prairie burns. The injun worked for him all the way. You work, and I work, and now we go felling trees for Pedersen here without thinking about our own livelihood. Surely we've got to think about getting ourselves through the winter."

"Yes, or more rightly put, we're supposed to get *you* through it. If you don't want to be here you can clear out. Who's asked you for anything? When you get tired of doing something you can stop getting food and disappear."

"There, there, Rasmus, a person's also supposed to think a little bit about himself, and you don't do that. Pedersen took the best homestead here - well - he hasn't quite *got* it yet..."

Rasmus took a step closer.

"Not *got* it?"

"Other people have their rights too, I guess," Jensen mumbled. "Why should he have the best one?"

"Because he opened his mouth first. And now that's what *I'm* doing. Watch out you don't take papers on Pedersen's homestead or I'll mangle you. And that land over there to the southwest between those two split hills, you know, that's *mine*."

Rasmus started loading, and it looked to Jensen as though the conversation had ended. He coughed a couple of times in preparation. Everything always seemed to go to pieces whenever he was going to say something. Rasmus never really understood what he meant, Jensen thought, and that was the trouble...

As a matter of fact things had become quite homelike on the hillside, where they had dug themselves in for the time being. Thin logs formed a roof out over the hollow; on top of them was an entire haystack. Other logs were stuck into the ground in front so that there was only a narrow entrance. The floor was strewn thickly with grass. The chickens cackled on the hill, and the rooster was master in Beaver Coulee. Nicoline grasped the situation and didn't eat the chickens. She hassled the coyotes in the valleys when the moon was up, but even so must have let herself be charmed by her archenemy, thought Rasmus. Eventually no one could doubt it, for finally Nicoline herself delivered the proof in the shape of five blind huskies which were dug out by Rasmus from an old badger hole. "That's too crude! We don't need to breed that damned brood. Wild huskies are worse than any of those they have come from - ugh, Nicoline! To think that you'd want to have anything to do with that howling vermin which has such poor taste that they would want to have anything to do with *you*, you singed monster."

But Nicoline was worse than the coyote mothers who simply ran over on to a hill and watched someone take their litter. She suddenly fastened on to Rasmus's throat. He let the pups go, grabbed Nicoline around the neck with both hands and squeezed hard, throttling her before she could tear open his throat. After he threw Nicoline down over the hill, he staggered a moment, and then gathered up the pups and killed them. He picked up a stone to crush the forehead of the lifeless Nicoline, but she slid off suddenly like a shadow into the grass.

Nicoline didn't come back. She joined the coyotes, and they heard her bellow with them at the rising moon. Charles shook his head when he found that out: - "I hope somebody's lucky enough to shoot Nicoline, for otherwise there'll be misfortune. There's bad blood in that dog, but it's too good for the coyotes."

Rasmus had a swollen neck for a long time, but he didn't do anything about the wounds, and they gradually healed. But the white scars came to follow him his whole life. Later he hated even the thought of Nicoline, and that was the reason he learned to shoot. At some point that episode would cost Nicoline her life.

By the hollow the children played with animals and flowers. They were happy, for now they were immune to mosquito bites. They didn't think they were in Paradise, but they were. The horses came running many times a day, frightened whenever the botflies tried to get into their nostrils. They stuck their heads into the door and got a quiet glow in their wet eyes - so we escaped this time! The children played between the legs of the horses, and the animals stepped carefully beside them. Pedersen stroked his beard and laughed. Indeed, they had come to sunny Alberta.

His house began to take shape under their hands. The floor was made of raw logs with clay stamped into the grooves, raw logs through and through, a large, square box with a mountain of turf on top. For days they sweated over the door and the stove, solving the problems with stones and with those experiences which had been collected along the way. Theodor had to have the light work the whole time; he filled all the holes of the nest with moss.

Now that so much had been accomplished, they started on a house for Rasmus. He had chosen a place in front of a little grove of trees on one of the valley slopes. But then Jensen became very gloomy - they'd taken all the best places, what was he going to be left with?

"Are we supposed to find it for you?" asked Rasmus. "Don't you have eyes yourself? Here are many thousands of square miles, you nitwit, and then you complain about too little space - I wish there were."

But Jensen continued in a completely different train of thought.

"I've been reckoning on our building together."

"Isn't that what we're doing too?"

"But, we two. Like in partnership..."

Rasmus began whistling to end the discussion. Jensen could get plenty of help for his house-building without even asking - Rasmus didn't give another thought at all to what the other one actually meant.

They needed various things, and early one morning Jensen drove to town. He didn't come back until dusk and was quite silent. The work progressed until Rasmus too had his house roofed in. Then he arranged with Pedersen to go to town and get homestead papers.

Jensen walked around restlessly while they were away. He took long walks up on the prairie and down through the coulees. He replied absent-mindedly whenever the children asked him about something. By noon he was inside Rasmus's house where he had already been living for several days. He felt the walls critically and sighed. It was a really good house...

Toward afternoon the wagon appeared up on the prairie. Each of the boys took one of the little girls and ran to meet their father. But both men were strangely silent. Pedersen cast a sidelong glance, half frightened and half curious, at Rasmus; there was a look of expectation in the old fellow's faun eyes. The boys also became silent and looked apprehensively from one to the other. They didn't recognize Rasmus at all - there was no doubt it was he, but his whole manner boded disaster. Mouth and eyes were screwed up. To be sure his face was flushed as always, but even so he looked unnaturally pale.

"Where's Jensen?" he asked when they were equally far from each of the houses.

"He's with us," said Frederik.

Rasmus jumped off.

"Tell him to come to me. I'm going up above my house. And he's not to keep me waiting!"

The wagon drove on. When it was quite a distance from Rasmus, the boys began to question their father. But he just grunted in his beard. They got no answer. Neither of the boys uttered a word when they came in, and then eventually Pedersen said,

"By the way, you're supposed to go up to Rasmus's. He's on the prairie above his house, and he said that he didn't want to wait too long."

Jensen was ill at ease. Pedersen didn't meet his eyes, but the boys stared at him as at one condemned to death.

"That's really strange," mumbled Jensen.

Pedersen didn't answer. Jensen hesitated a bit

"What do you think he wants with me, Pedersen?"

"It's none of my business."

That answer didn't comfort Jensen. But he went. He didn't hurry, and the three pairs of eyes that followed him saw that he paused many times on the way.

Down in the coulee out of sight Rasmus sat, waiting on a stone. His glance stayed glued to Jensen from the moment he came up over the crest of the hill, but he remained sitting.

Jensen looked over his head,

"What do you want me for?"

"Why have you taken my homestead?"

"I haven't done that at all," said Jensen. His voice trembled a bit. "It's just a service I've done for you, Rasmus. And of course you saved that money."

"And you got the homestead?"

Jensen became more certain.

"Good lord, Rasmus, it's only like that on paper. It doesn't make any difference whose name is there. If anything it was a surprise for you, Rasmus. For we two bachelors, hee, hee, we have plenty of room with one house...we, you know, we'll avoid a lot of inconvenience..."

Then it dawned on Rasmus that Jensen was after much more than just the homestead. He wanted to have Rasmus and the house as well. An almost hysterical laughter escaped him. But he immediately became serious.

"I'll tell you something, Jensen. I took you up here to kill you. But now I think you'd better be content with a thrashing. For of all the fools in Canada and the U.S. you're the biggest one. Come here, little Jensen."

Jensen took a step back.

"Rasmus, have you gone completely mad? Can't you understand that..."

Rasmus jumped up.

"Stop!"

But Jensen ran. In a few leaps Rasmus caught up with him, grabbed him by the chest with one hand and swung his right hand toward him. Jensen screamed. Then Rasmus shook the man and flung him down.

Jensen got up. But Rasmus was already on the way home. Jensen followed him slowly. Behind him Nicoline came out from a thicket and looked thoughtfully down into the coulee. Her mutilated tail writhed like a cat's.

- - -

Rasmus walked down into one of the side valleys and got his oxen. Afterward in front of his house he fashioned an ingenious combination of chains and poles which he connected to the harness. Then he hitched the oxen to the house. There was room enough on the prairie, but damn it he was going to take his house along with him. He measured the lengths of chain one more time, lifted the harness, tightened or loosened it here and there. Now it should be right. Then he climbed up onto the roof, shoveled all the grass turf down and let his whip fall. The oxen strained, and the house with all of Rasmus Dansker's wordly goods, chickens, benches, tables and stove, slid slowly down into the bottom of the valley.

Jensen had seated himself up on a slope and was looking on. Pedersen and his boys kept themselves indoors. It was undoubtedly best not to see anything - officially. Rasmus roared at the oxen and got the house to slide again. Now they headed north. Even after darkness had fallen, his gruff, fiery shouting could be heard.

In the morning the house stood in a narrow valley behind a large flat area. Here it was easy to make a driveway up to the prairie; Pedersen saw that at once. Not a bad place at all. Heh, heh! Jensen had made a fine mess for himself. He certainly wouldn't get Rasmus to fetch logs for his house.

Toward morning Jensen came. He stood modestly inside the door a while and didn't say anything. Rasmus was lying in the hay over in the corner reading a grisly murder story which he would soon be able to rattle off by heart standing on one leg. He let the book sink and looked stiffly at Jensen.

"What kind of a ninepin are you?" he asked inhospitably.

47

"This is really silly, Rasmus. And just when it was going so well..."

"You have a couple of boxes standing here full of junk. Get them off my homestead."

"Don't do it," said Jensen. "It will be a completely meaningless expense for you."

"First of all it was my money, secondly it's paid, thirdly it's none of your business. Get out!"

Jensen got a sinking feeling in his knees.

"I thought then...that when you'd become yourself...I could live here."

"You have your own homestead."

"Well, but Rasmus, there's no house there now."

"No, there isn't. But it wasn't long ago you lived in a hole. And yesterday you almost came to live in a much worse hole. Be happy with your homestead."

"Can't you see then, Rasmus...two can go farther than one."

I can go farthest without *you*. Clear out!"

"Can I borrow your oxen then?" asked Jensen desperately.

"Nix! I'm going to get logs for one more room. Necessary expansion. Clear out!"

"But..."

Rasmus got up.

"Clear out!"

He ran toward the door, and Jensen went flying outside. His boxes came crashing after him. Jensen carried one of them a short distance. Then he let it stand and got the other one which he carried somewhat farther. After that he went back after the first one. So it was that Erik Jensen moved from Rasmus's over to Pedersen's and gave up any further attempt at collaborating with anybody.

8.

When Rasmus had said he wanted to expand it was not a pretense - simply because he didn't use pretenses. After his mind had quieted down from his earlier rows with the crafty Jensen, he had gone to bed and read his novel. he did read, but his thoughts travelled far away anyway, taking the road back to a ranch near Youngstown. When they had reached that far, they became too interesting for him to be able to read at the same time. He recollected everything Eva had said from her first hello until she placed her firm hand in his for goodbye. Then we'll see each other in the spring. He opened his eyes - and knew at that moment two things - that there should be one more room and that Jensen was peering into the door. An hour later he rode to the forest and began felling timber.

There was happiness in his dwelling. He could give expression to his joy in song, as it was nobody's concern that he sang poorly. Theodor often came to his place, sitting with a serious air and listening to all the astounding stories Rasmus told. And Rasmus always talked when Theodor was there. For he liked him.

Theodor gradually grew more ill. It didn't seem to help him that he had come to a new climate.

"I know very well I'm going to die soon," he said. Rasmus was at a loss. Here was something he couldn't take care of and put in order without further ado.

And Rasmus toiled on with his house. He placed the new one a short distance from the other one and built over the space between them. It was rough and low of course, but when one day he stood back a little and inspected his work critically, he saw that it fitted in with the coulee. Everything was exceedingly good.

The furniture would be worked on indoors during the winter...now ground had to be broken. And Rasmus got himself a plow in town. From down in the coulee they saw him plowing with the oxen on the prairie. Everyone had to go up and see. Jensen sighed. He realized clearly now how Rasmus had cheated him. That's the way the world was. See how the rich earth was turning behind the plodding oxen. And Rasmus, he was a real nobleman - of course he couldn't walk even if the old wornout plow was designed for that. He had lashed sticks and gadgets on to it so he could sit there with fancy airs. As for Pedersen, he looked up into the sky. Here the plow wasn't followed by swarms of gulls. Yes, that's right; he was far into the great mainland - in sunny Alberta.

- - -

Pedersen too got his plow into the ground, and each evening they had to ride over each other's land to see how it was going. Jensen had a nice plan about partnership with Pedersen, and Pedersen had nodded and said yah and well - and made Jensen feel secure. But it was preferable that Jensen not feel secure, for then he bit off more than he could chew, and at last Pedersen stroked his beard rouguishly - nah, no, *papers*? Division? No, indeed, he didn't want that. It was money thrown away, and that wasn't why he had come here - to sunny Alberta!

Jensen scratched the back of his neck despondently. He couldn't very well say of course, "Remember that I am an old man." For Pedersen was two years older. And what did he really know about that drying of money back east? Oh yes, one was poorly situated.

It ended with Pedersen's asking what, everything considered, did Jensen want here? Why didn't he build on his own homestead? Certainly he had not thought about living with Pedersen the whole winter, too? Jensen squirmed. Two men always got more out of a thing than one. "Yes, except food," said Pedersen. "You'd better go back to the States."

But Jensen stayed. Each day Pedersen became a trifle more brusque. His plan was working though, sort of, thought Jensen - and such an otherwise reasonable man would after all be very likely to discover what served his best interests.

Jensen had got an idea. He cut hay. It was actually best on Rasmus's and Pedersen's land - was not nearly so good elsewhere. But when he ventured into some marshy stretches on Rasmus's homestead, Rasmus threw stones, and his aim was good. Then Jensen tried it on Pedersen's land. But Pedersen came and asked gruffly who was supposed to have that hay? If it wasn't being cut for him, he would appreciate it if it were just left standing. But Jensen wanted it largely for himself. He dreamed about a corner in hay. The others would probably not have time for it, and when winter came - then they would certainly be willing to negotiate. He cut more on his own land, but it was definitely poorer here. It billowed far more temptingly at the others'. Strange that they had got

50

exactly those two places where there was something that was good. And sadly he continued cutting hay on the homestead which had been worth so much while Rasmus had wanted it.

Pedersen and Rasmus were busy turning large tracts of land. However tired Pedersen was when he came home, he laughed with the children. Oh yes, what land. And a railroad would come here in two years. He began to say vespers and was still laughing in his beard when he fell asleep. Sunny Alberta! And his plow never stood still as long as it was light. Frederik and his father took turns at the plow. Rasmus stayed at home and began cutting hay. Day after day he moved forward with arched back over the meadows, or he pulled the hay together into stacks. From sunup he bent tirelessly over the scythe. Jensen completely lost his good humour. What is one supposed to do with hay when one can't corner the market in it?

- - -

And the coulee changed. Its hues passed into the more subdued grays and browns. When Rasmus went down to his house in the evening he looked out over the valleys: It was a beautiful land even now, as autumn entered Beaver Coulee. Gossamer spider webs sailed through the air in the valleys on dewy mornings. It became chilly at night, but one toiled all the more to get the blood moving.

On those cold mornings when Rasmus scanned the area from a peephole up toward the prairie, he saw Nicoline. She was too far away to be shot from here. Oh, how he hated that animal. Not for that bite in the throat - that was over and done with. He himself didn't actually know what it was. But at any rate he couldn't stand the fact - that much he realized - that this former coyote-hater now hung around with the coyotes. There was treachery and scheming in it, and now Nicoline was probably hiding a litter of huskies somewhere on the prairie. Later more would come. A lovely prospect. He would prefer not to have Eva come to Beaver Coulee as long as Nicoline was alive.

Eva -? Don't be so sure, Rasmus, do you really think you'll get her, will she follow you out to your homestead? Isn't there a flock of greedy cowboys on the ranch, isn't she worth desiring, and what do you know about her feelings? He became melancholy. It had been foolish of him to leave Youngstown without getting a proper answer. Was there anything strange in her mentioning their seeing each other in the spring. He had probably said it himself twenty times that day? Hadn't she smiled when she said it? Could she have been laughing at him from the window when they left? Oh, Eva. Will you have taken another man by the time I come riding to Youngstown? I wonder if you were already someone else's? Yes, he had been stupid. Why did it have to wait till spring? She could just as well be here now.

With hot eyes he looked around the room. Yes, she should have been here now.

- - -

Thick frost began to collect during the nights. The coulee lay glaringly white in the morning, and when he went out before the sun had chased the frost away, he saw Nicoline's tracks on the hillcrests. Wait, Nicoline, until there's new-fallen snow. I'll ferret you out along with your damned brood. Eva will not see your grinning face.

Again he put his plow to the earth. Perhaps a lot could be gained before the frost came. In the rimy mornings the newly broken strip of earth lay behind him like a sore in the land, a sore from which crops would rise. And he thought again about Eva, Eva...

Pedersen came over one day. He was busy plowing and visited only rarely, but now he wanted to include Rasmus in on a deal. He'd like a cow for the sake of the children, and anyhow he noticed himself that he needed it. It wasn't good to be constantly eating animal fat. Rasmus counted his money. He probably had enough for one. Yes, that was true enough, one ought to have a cow. And they went to town and came home with cows.

That same day Jensen was turned out by Pedersen. "Now you've had enough time to consider, Jensen. Perhaps it's not right that I don't tell you until now, winter being so close, but you've heard it often enough, and I really thought you'd have gone by now. I have children, and besides that I know now that you're richer than I am. You could have had a house on your homestead and a good start for spring. But that's your headache. You've got to leave today."

Jensen pleaded for mercy, but Pedersen laughed and stroked his beard. "No, no, little Jensen. After all you can stay at a hotel, Jensen. I've had enough of you."

Jensen walked out and looked at his hay. Hay! He had enough of that...

That night he stayed in their first hole. The day after that he felled trees in Indian Forest. He toiled as none of the others had done. He went ahead like wildfire. And when the snow came, Jensen was under a roof on his homestead.

Rasmus felt one morning how quiet it had become in the land. And when he opened the door, the air struck against him with a raw, new smell like that of iron. The valleys were clad in snow. He took his rifle and walked up to follow Nicoline's tracks. They stood out clearly enough. For four hours he followed them, followed them in an enormous circle, down into the coulees and up again - and he ended up standing at his own door. The fresh tracks went up to the dog's old observation post. He cursed under his breath. Nicoline had taunted him. He wanted to ride over and talk to Charles about the matter. If anyone could take care of Nicoline it had to be he. Finally he went in and ate. It would be delightful to get the better of the beast. Last night the whole hoard had been crowing up here with Nicoline leading them all. Ugh, how nasty that was of Nicoline!

9.

The first days after the snow came Theodor felt better, but it was only a short respite. His large eyes shone cheerlessly from the box, and his cough was bad. Pedersen was hanging his head when Rasmus came. "Well, things are going badly with Theodor. I was almost too old, and he was too sick when we came to Alberta, you know. Now he's laid up. Oh Lord."

The rest of that day Rasmus walked around in the coulees kicking the snow. He wouldn't put up with this. He didn't want to see that young fellow lie dying. Something had to be done. Rasmus scratched his head. Of course he wasn't a doctor. If only he could remember a little of what he had heard about tuberculosis. A nasty illness. Rasmus had a vague idea of something about fresh air and wind, straight back and deep breathing. But of course it wasn't such a simple matter when the boy was too tired to walk. And you *couldn't* have such a young fellow dying, that much was certain. Still pondering, Rasmus kept sauntering around. If only he had his mother's doctor book now. There was power in it. Whenever someone had been sick and the book's directions had been too complicated to be understood, she had read it aloud by the sickbed - with the same ring and unction as when she'd read from the Bible. It would be sure to help. Mother hadn't been a foolish person.

Suddenly Rasmus stood still, and shortly afterward he was on the way to Pedersen's. He went in and sat down on Theodor's bed.

"I'll tell you something, my boy. We must see about getting you cured. Whatever cures a smith kills a tailor, but you're no tailor..."

His voice was gentle like a mother's when he bent down over Theodor and slowly continued:

"You're very sick. And you're a peach of a fellow, you are. You don't blubber over your number being up. But I don't think anyone will die as long as they don't want to if death isn't downright hanging over them. And here of course we have time enough to think things over. There's fresh air which is necessary. Whenever I've slept outside during the winter and have had enough clothes on me, I have waked up feeling as fit as ever. I can make a house just outside here - from really solid logs with a tight roof jutting out over the walls. But on the upper part of the walls every second board must be removed. In there you're to lie in a box in the middle of the floor when you can't be up. You must never venture under a roof in any other place until you're well..."

Rasmus broke off. Theodor's hand sought his.

"Do you think it could help?"

"It's helped the four cases I've heard about," declared Rasmus.

He had never heard the slightest bit about even one case.

Theodor's fingers squeezed more tightly. Suddenly he cried.

"I tell you I've hardened myself," he sobbed, "because I thought there was no hope."

"Indeed! You can swear that there is. It's just that it's strong medicine."

Theodor's eyes lit up.

"When can that house be made, Rasmus?"

"Well, we'll get it done quickly. I have a sled, so we can get logs. Your father and I will go over and cut down trees tomorrow..."

Pedersen had been sitting rocking on a chair. He avoided looking Theodor in the eye.

"Well, it is certainly good that Rasmus found a way," he said. "And we have both hay and blankets. You can have a splendid nest in that house. Ha, ha, little Theodor, you'll be a perfect watchman to have outside here, you know."

Theodor raised himself on his elbow; he saw life returning. Rasmus got up and walked home. His throat tightened a bit. If it went well - that was of course fine and good - but, good Lord, if it didn't...

Down in the bottom of the valley he stood still and looked steadily up toward his house. Outside the door sat Nicoline.

For a long time he stood looking up at the dog. Nicoline was very smart: Rasmus didn't have his rifle along. He considered many possibilities. Could he possibly lure the dog into a trap? Charles had to be consulted. That damned coyote whore! He'd be careful from now on to close his door before he left.

The building of the house for Theodor went quickly, and the boy was pathetically happy when Rasmus carried him out into the new dwelling. "Now you'll see, my boy, that we'll get the better of the poison in you. Everything that's wrong with you will blow away, and finally there'll be nothing left - and nothing is going to get into you again. That's the whole thing. Fresh air is necessary!"

When it got dark, neither he nor Pedersen could quite leave him. The moon rose and shone in, the broad shadows of the house beams lay boldly in the white light. Theodor laughed. "I do thank you, Rasmus. I can already notice that it's helping."

They left. When they were well away, Theodor crept deep down into his nest and cried. But later his face surfaced again, composed and calm. The shadow cut across his head so that there was only a white, narrow-lipped mouth and near it a hand. There he lay looking out where the hills spread like enormous, jagged theatre wings with sterile iron blue shadows. In the sheet-white night the coldness of the firmament descended onto the earth. The planks creaked as the frost slammed its jaws. He felt the atmosphere of the sea over the hilly prairie and became so lonely. It was as if a great calm voice were speaking out there. Death, winter had risen in white clothes and hung over Alberta. But Theodor's lips narrowed: He wanted to live.

The cold became crueller as night passed. And by midnight he heard the hare's child-like cry; the coyotes were upon it. A little later Nicoline shrieked, quite close. It was as if there were an agreement that she would whine alone; not a single yelp did the coyotes give in answer. Nicoline kept it up, and Theodor's glance became a rigid stare. There was more than just death in her voice, there was sorrow and misery, all the ill-fated spirits of the prairie - there was a flood of coagulated blood through Beaver Coulee, a white corpse with plucked out eyes revolving in the black current.

And Nicoline shrieked. With her wails she summoned departed generations from the earth. Bent over, they rose up from the snow and saw that people had come who could be tormented.

But then she abruptly fell silent. From somewhere came laughter, raw and echoing as if it were the night itself which opened its mouth and set the darkness resounding. When it ended Nicoline gave up her sorcery, became content to howl for corpses with her gaping mouth. Was that the signal? Now the coyotes gained their power of speech

Close by, rifle shots suddenly cracked. And Theodor felt how those sounds helped him up through an abyss of madness. Finally a sound that announced people of flesh and blood...

There were several shots. Then he heard Rasmus's voice:

"Are you asleep, Theodor?"

"No, gosh, did they kick up a row!"

"I thought I'd got Nicoline. But no, not this time. But I caught the owl anyway. You must have heard it laughing?"

A burden fell from Theodor's mind. Naturally it had been the big horned owl laughing. Still the night became all too big and quiet when Rasmus left.

- - -

57

Jensen had looked sourly at the building going on over at Pedersen's. Hard enough that a person should be kept ignorant of what was happening right around his own homestead. But he would certainly not go poking his nose into it, they should not think that of him, those fine folk! Thought they were something, that was the whole thing. They weren't the least bit better than anybody else.

But since the house was standing there he would go over and have a look at any rate. From a distance his eyes were fastened on that piece of architecture - *that* must be one of Rasmus's ideas. What in heaven's name had they thought of using that castle for? Were they going to catch owls in it?

Jensen was shaken down to his soul when he heard the explanation and saw it was serious. "But, dear Pedersen, surely you can understand that that Rasmus will kill Theodor. That's clear enough. Good Lord, the poor boy. No, I'd never have thought you could go along with that, Pedersen. After all it's pure blasphemy."

Pedersen looked up heavily, but he slowly stroked his beard and said,

"Blasphemy? Then you must be happy, you who are a freethinker. Other-wise you'd have come and given better advice while Theodor was on the point of dying on us."

Loudly he added,

"Now the boy's getting better. Thank God we found a way."

Jensen comprehended only too well that those words were not directed to him. However, he began to answer just as loudly:

"So you believe *that*..."

He stopped abruptly. In two seconds old Pedersen had come to resemble a grizzly bear who has risen up on his hind legs. Jensen saw two arms lift up. They were more massive than he had ever before considered possible and were placed on his shoulders not as arms but as organic extensions on his body. He fell back.

"What...what...would you strike an old man?" he whispered - for he under-stood that whatever happened he had to speak *softly*. He was in the habit of being an old man and in his hurry had completely forgotten that Pedersen had been through a couple of seasons more than he himself.

Then Pedersen's bulk settled down; he laughed through his beard.

"What's the matter, Jensen? I was just stretching. But you're a freethinker and probably like that guy Cain who couldn't see anything without believing he was going to be put to death. Heh, heh, you're a queer fellow, Jensen! Oh, no, I won't dispose of you before I'm sure about your last will and testament."

Jensen glowered. He cursed Rasmus in his heart. Here he was an old man, and had to see to it that his old age would be free from worry, and now he was to be punished for being thrifty - now he had to pay where before he had been given a helping hand. Here they had dragged him to a wild land, others got their land plowed, but he didn't, he only got hay which no one valued, and he didn't even have any animals to eat it. Wouldn't it have been more natural for them to buy his hay than go to the bother of cutting it themselves? That was his opinion anyway.

10.

Rasmus had been out with his rifle to see if he could catch a glimpse of Nicoline. He went far toward the southwest to one of the frozen marshes which lay on the prairie. The dog's tracks led out among the reeds on the ice, accompanied by those of a coyote.

While Rasmus was riding, he suddenly forgot what he was doing out there. He pulled up his horse and looked around carefully. The marsh was full of muskrat lodges - halleluja! Here was money to be earned! He turned his horse around at once and rode home, his mind occupied with thoughts of traps.

Frederik came up to him and looked mystified at Rasmus's handiwork, small boxes with trapdoors. Do you suppose Rasmus wanted to catch mice? He went home to tell his father, who appeared shortly afterward. He smelled profit and cast a sidelong glance at the traps while talking about the weather. "Hm, well. Theodor is still in the same old condition, luckily not worse. Are you going to catch sparrows?"

He was on guard with his eyes, but Rasmus acted as if nothing were going on and simply answered no. He wasn't going to catch sparrows. And it was best Pedersen didn't catch *him* right away either. Ought to see first if there were many of those muskrats. Rasmus laughed to himself, ha, *muskrats*! Perhaps by spring there'd be money for more implements than he had dared hope.

That evening there were northern lights over Beaver Coulee. Two pale light bridges stood arched under the Big Dipper which pointed down on them with its handle. Smoke rose quietly from the houses in the valley. Rasmus studied the weather. It would very likely be fine tomorrow for going out with his traps.

During the night it grew colder until there was almost no escaping it. And then it was blowing. When it got light there was a storm. The snow rushed through the valleys like smoking steam. A roving coyote came close to Rasmus's house in the gray morning, hungry and restless in its movements. Rasmus shot it and wished it had been Nicoline. Clouds gathered, new snow began to fall.

The prairie became different and yet the same as it lay out there with its short horizon. The storm's intensity increased. Wherever it blew up it began like a harpist who used the hills as strings; around one of them it screamed like horses running in frozen snow - then the wind shouted over to the next hill and bellowed around it, moaned and continued on to the next rise. One gust of wind could be heard following another through the coulee, each with its own sound, a sea of sound with swelling waves. One always knew how far each gust of wind had come, heard it force its whistling way into the valley, mark its course and slip back out.

The coulee changed shape and colour again from hour to hour. The light shifted and the drifts went wandering. Eternally unchangeable was Beaver Coulee, but never the same. It whispered about everything that a mortal man has ever dreamed and seen, it was Denmark, it was Mount Everest, it was the moon's dead craters. But first and last and in all eternity: Beaver Coulee.

When the somber day was on the point of turning into night the storm suddenly became silent. It was as though all its wailing emissaries had suddenly regained their composure, stood still and then, thoughtful, gone their way, ashamed of how witlessly they had betrayed their bestial nature. It was quite still out there. Rasmus emerged, stood in the middle of a drift and looked at the valley, seeing the drifting snow silently settle on the ground. God only knew how Theodor was in his open cage; he was probably lying under a snow drift, but fortunately it was so cold that it wouldn't melt. Better go over and see how he was getting along...

Then without warning a hailstorm broke loose as if the lid of Hell had burst open. A hurricane roared through the valleys with its lap full of ice. It looked as if a hill a short way from Rasmus would be dug up by its roots. Branches, earth and snow flew from it like smoke. A minute later the valley was full of whirling snow. Heaven preserve us, thought Rasmus and slipped inside, it damned well looks like we've come to sunny Alberta! You could downright wish you were safe and sound at home with mother and the pig.

He crept into his box while the storm wailed out there. His fire went out, but he lay in the darkness and was comfortable. What luck that you're a gifted person with a sleeping box and all modern conveniences! It would have been a pretty kettle of fish if you were a mangy coyote with frost-bitten paws, sheltered behind a snowdrift. Heaven's punishment is upon you, Nicoline. You could have been lying here between my legs and had it so lovely. Now instead you can warm your lecherous heart on a lump of ice while the cold stings you, as if you had gone backwards into your coat, for it is written that the wages of sin are death, you miserable cousin of a skunk.

Very soon the cold hammered its way into the cabin. The ice advanced

61

through ceiling and walls, approached the stove in a wedge over from the door, grew up from the floor, spread like mould out over the rugs, rimed his hair, coloured the stove white. Rasmus turned and made himself cozy in the warmth of the bed. Here you really found out what a nest was. Thank the Lord for the bed! First four feet of delicious hay, then a sack of birchbark, next yourself, then woolen blankets and another sack of hay on the top. Wasn't he well provided for, heh, heh, in sunny Alberta!

Toward midnight there was a knock on the door. Wide awake, Rasmus stuck his red nose out from the blankets.

"Who is it?"

"It's me - Charles. I'm tired."

"The door isn't locked."

Charles jerked it loose; it had been frozen stuck. Rasmus got a candle lit, and the Metis' gigantic figure stepped forward in the circle of light. He had a frozen coyote hanging over his shoulder.

"I was down south," he explained. "Have been outside several days. Then came the bad weather, and now I'd like to stay overnight."

He threw off his clothes and went into the box with Rasmus. They rolled themselves into the blankets and lay like a twin mummy. Charles stretched, "Ah!" But he was too tall for the bed, and Rasmus cried out, "You'll push the end off the box!"

Rasmus let the candle burn a moment, the wind came in, the flame drifted here and there, shadows ran on the log walls which were white with frost. Outside the storm blustered. Then Rasmus blew out the candle, and it became pitch dark. For a moment a green worm slid over his eyelid.

"One could build another house outside of this one," said Rasmus eventually. "Then you wouldn't get a snowstorm right in through the door."

Charles didn't answer immediately. But then he said,

"The house is good enough until you've gathered in your first harvest. What you need is something quite different. I would have thought that one more person would be in the caravan before we left Youngstown."

Rasmus didn't understand immediately the meaning of that remark. But then he began to talk about Eva calmly and quietly.

"I don't really understand it," he said, "for of course I scarcely know her. But anyway I think I have known her for many years. What can cause a thing like that? I've felt like that several times. The first time was in the old country when I was a boy of seven going to school. A new girl came into the class, a little one with long, dark curls. I had a collection of picture postcards at home, and I immediately took them along to school for her. And I put flowers in her school bag when she wasn't looking. Then she moved with her parents again. I wonder what can have become of a little curlyhead like that? The next one, she was blonde - the first one was dark, you see - I was thirteen then. She had an underbite, it was basically pretty. It made her look so shy and innocent. But nothing ever came of it with her, for when you're thirteen you're not so quick on the trigger as you were when you were seven. And now with Eva - it's exactly the same. The more you have to say the less you get said. As a matter of fact it's strange, don't you think?"

"One should just get oneself a girl and be quiet," said Charles. "It's just one's imagination that one is supposed to have a lot to say to her, sort of a kind of sensation in the skin. Woman is a religion. One says a whole lot to Venus, but she doesn't understand anything. She's a vision."

That sounded to Rasmus almost as erudite as when freethinker Jensen referred to the scriptures. But of course it had some connection with Eva, and thus it was interesting.

"I want to ride to Youngstown when I have finished sowing this spring. But I can't deny that I'm somewhat nervous. - What can you know about what she's doing?"

Full of thoughts of love, Rasmus talked on. Charles said nothing. It was very pleasant to have a silent listener so he talked on and on. Then Rasmus suddenly understood by his deep, breathing sounds that Charles was asleep.

"Good Lord," thought Rasmus, "of course he's dead tired. I didn't even offer him a bit of food..."

Rasmus lay awake for a while longer listening to the storm roaring in the valleys and throwing itself against the log wall like a battering ram. Then his consciousness separated into two parts; something sank down into sleep, something else was awake, and the world turned into images. While the storm's booming was still casting spells somewhere in his brain, the coulee glided forth in summer colours into his field of vision, with gossipping springs along the sides of the valley and flowers nodding to each other. A cloud drifted through the great valley. It was white and slowly turned about itself. A short way from Rasmus's cabin it rose in a whirling white spiral until something happened which he had foreseen: - From the spiral of mist Eva was created, and she walked smiling toward him over the green grass. She was free and easy when she came to him in the cabin, not burdened by any shame. The flowers nodded in over the threshold after her. The sun left its course and came closer to the earth. A tropical forest with flaming baskets of flowers rose in Beaver Coulee. Sleeping, with a smile about his mouth, he whispered out into the darkness, "Sunny Alberta!"

- - -

Rasmus reflected a couple of minutes when he woke up in the morning, then flew from his box like a rocket and flung on his clothes, hopping about. The cold struck like a lash. When he was dressed, he ran back and forth to get his blood circulating, then started chopping firewood so rapidly that the pieces whizzed to all sides. Soon the fire was roaring in the stove. He went out and filled a bucket with snow, put it on the stove and was outside again, went up and down the snowdrifts, came in and began furiously sweeping with the broom. Charles lay in the bed following him seriously with his black eyes. "Cold, cold, cold," shouted Rasmus. It sounded like an exorcism, and it was, too. The cold was on its way into him and had to be shouted out. He stuffed sticks edgeways down into the stove and danced around again with his broom, sweeping snow, dirt and sticks from one end of the house to the other, back and forth, until he got a bright idea: He kicked off his boots and went under the blankets and haysack back to Charles.

It wasn't blowing so hard any more, but was snowing heavily. It drifted in through cracks and joints. Outdoors the field of vision ended ten paces away, you only saw a little, storming world. Here all hope had to be excluded. It would never, never be summer again.

The stove became black and wet in the midst of all the white, but farther away the warmth was having little effect. Rasmus had got out of the bed a couple of times, filled up the bucket with snow, and crammed several sticks into the stove. It had stood glowing for a couple of hours before the ice flora died in the cabin. Then the two got up and made breakfast.

Rasmus questioned Charles about how one could get at Nicoline, "for I tell you - either Nicoline is going to leave Beaver Coulee or I will. It's no use your asking me. That dog is a plague. I'll go mad having it running around loose. Today of course you can't see, but every morning she's standing up on the prairie glaring down here. I've tried to shoot her from here, but of course it would be extraordinary luck if I could do it. What does she want?"

"She just sticks around. Such a dog may have had many masters and been wild three or four times. But she can't really be either wild or tame. That's why she has to look down here. Besides I've come to think that Nicoline has coyote blood in her. One of her parents was husky. Such a mixture of coyote, poodle and terrier and God knows what can degenerate into something bad. You can't say she's smarter than people, for her smartness is a completely different kind, but Nicoline is a crafty thing. We'll get her one day. You'll never catch Nicoline in a trap, but one day one of us will run across her with a rifle."

That didn't console Rasmus. And there was one more thing - Nicoline's howling was now often heard over at Pedersen's. It scared Theodor. He didn't say anything, but Rasmus knew it. Rasmus was disappointed in Charles. There couldn't be anything wrong except that Charles wasn't in the mood. Charles! He could go right up on the prairie and get Nicoline if he only wanted to.

11.

Winter didn't loosen its hold again. Now and then the sun appeared, but it made no promises. It was distant and cold, sailing low. Later in the morning it could be so cold that you expected the valleys to burst. In clear weather the air hung full of glittering ice needles. Then the coyotes' tracks covered the wide plains, inscriptions of restlessness and hunger. All day long Rasmus was out hunting for coyote and muskrats. He garnered in the middle of the bitter winter, for he couldn't just keep quiet inside; he wasn't capable of hibernating. Jensen was different. He lay in his sleeping box for whole weeks at a time, sucking his teeth or gnawing on the straw of his bedding. He was phlegmatic. Each day Pedersen trudged around an hour or so in with Theodor who lay coughing with several feet of snow about him. Pedersen would look at him out of the corner of his eye. This was truly a drastic remedy. Theodor didn't say anything. His eyes thoughtfully followed his father. It was all right as long as it was day. But he dreaded the nights... Pedersen was bored, though he did more than Jensen, who by no means found time hanging heavy on his hands. He lay in his box hatching out high-flying plans. If spring came in good time now, and it probably would, he could get a lot plowed and readied without having to sow too late. He could easily borrow Pedersen's plow. It would be senseless to buy one while there was one standing around out here not being used. He could probably get pulling power. Jensen was an optimist. But if the others hadn't realized that you ought to be two on a farm, then *he* at least realized it. Yes indeed. He knew well enough what was going to happen. When he was through with the sowing, he'd buy something or other, a coloured scarf or even an elegant hat with ostrich feathers on it, and armed like this he'd go on a courting trip to Youngstown. He didn't take it seriously that Eva, to put it bluntly, had given him a clout. She was somewhat hot-headed, but there was good use for hot-headedness here, indeed there was! And it was just the proper time to get married. She was suitably young, and he was suitably old. A splendid match.

Perhaps a bit of cash would be a better idea than the gift? Well, one could never know of course what she would throw money away on.

Jensen reached out, got hold of a half eaten hare and gnawed along its backbone, as though he were playing a Jew's harp. He put the hare back and took a mouthful of snow to wash it down with. Hm, yes, a splendid match. The children would certainly not be baptized. No tricks. Surely one was master in one's own house. Jensen scratched himself.

- - -

Winter, winter, eternal winter, winter for eternity. Barren frost storms howled on the prairie for weeks, and during the nights the owl's sterile laughter became sharper until gashes from it hung in the air of the valleys. Rasmus looked up at the prairie in the morning and saw that Nicoline was lean; there had been few rabbits and hare that year. The horses crunched about on snow which shrieked in agony. The black eagle sat on a rise with its wings sloping down like a cape; it was the most silent of all the animals. Prairie chickens walked near the house. They made deep passages for themselves in the snow and ran in them like moles while one bird stuck its head up and turned to see if the world were in order. When the flock of them flew up they didn't laugh like the owl, which has no heart. The hen shouted seven times, "stupid ass", and twelve times, "fool", if it weren't stopped by buckshot in the middle of the lesson.

Rasmus had become tired of melt water. He wanted to break a hole in the ice of the brook and get real water again, and so he made the time pass as long as that took. He cut holes in several places until he found out where there was deep water. It was blue gray and tasted of clay, but he got, as it were, firm ground under his feet from it - generally an earthy taste so that one felt convinced that the earth still existed. Snow always left him with an iron taste in his mouth.

The moment he got up from the ice he saw Nicoline. Their eyes met for an instant. Then she was off, not with her tail between her legs but straight up in the air. Rasmus snatched up his rifle and shot. The snow stood up in a little cloud around the dog, but she went on uninjured. Rasmus shot and shot again, but didn't hit this time either. He cursed fiercely and ran on. The dog didn't get along much more quickly than he in the deep snow. At several points she jumped straight up and down, rolled over, sank in. Rasmus shot again, this time with precise aim. For a couple of seconds he stared gaping; he had shot Nicoline's tail off at the root. Nicoline threw herself to one side, grabbed her tail and ran on. She wanted to take what was hers with her. Now she turned behind a long bush, and Rasmus ran to be that much closer when his archenemy showed herself again.

But he didn't get to see Nicoline any more in that round. The crust of snow broke under him, and as he plunged through, he saw the white valley become poisonous green like a sulphur oven. He came to again in the half-light down on a new layer in the ice. To get up the same way was impossible, and he had to dig himself obliquely up through the snow. It didn't take long, but when he resurfaced, Nicoline was gone. He ran over to the bush, found the trail, a bloody one, and followed it up the side of the valley. But this took time. He sank in several places up to his neck. When he worked his way completely up, Nicoline was not to be seen. Only a short distance from there the trail led back down into the valley. Then Rasmus struck himself on the forehead and admitted that Nicoline was smarter than he. "But now see if you're so smart that you can put a shot-off tail on again! It looks as though you'll have to be taken in small pieces. It wouldn't surprise me if you took your tail along to eat. Then maybe it'll grow back on you again, you vermin."

Angry, he went over and filled his bucket with the violently flowing water. Damned Nicoline!

- - -

Midwinter came, and the nights were bitterly long. Previously Jensen had been seen outside now and then, but now he had become completely asocial and never showed himself. One day, when Rasmus was trudging around back and forth in with Theodor, Pedersen came and expressed his uneasiness, "Maybe something's happened, someone should really go over and see, but of course Jensen couldn't stand visits, since then he always thought that you were trying to get on his good side, and then wanted something or other."

"He's hibernating," said Rasmus, "and anyway I don't care. That fool. He took my homestead as soon as I had a house on it."

"What if he's lying there dead now, Rasmus?"

"Well, I can't wake up the dead. And certainly there's time enough to bury him when he thaws out in the spring. Then I'll probably lend a hand. For we can't have him lying there stinking."

Pedersen wanted to say something, but he thought better of it and laughed. "Heh, that Jensen!"

- - -

But Jensen was neither completely nor almost dead. Food lasts a long time when you're phlegmatic and just lying in bed. Jensen did nothing but turn

69

around. When he got tired of lying on his left side he turned around onto his right. He consumed his meals lying on his back, and Sundays he celebrated by turning around on his stomach. It was a gentle existence. Jensen had solved a problem. He followed neither the broad nor the narrow path. He simply lay down and remained lying there.

Now and then he busied himself with the prospects for the spring. He began thinking that Eva of course had to have a father. A living father it was to be hoped. Perhaps he could lend a helping hand with a couple of work horses. That would only be reasonable when his daughter was provided for. Perhaps she had a little money which could be put away for a rainy day. You could say what you would, Eva wouldn't be cheated with that marriage. It was really an extraordinary idea he had had about giving her a gift. Serious intentions were in themselves a great gift. Actually he was surely somewhat too kind-hearted. She would be getting her own home. Jensen wore a fish-like look and scratched himself.

He was lost in daydreams while the weather went wailing through Beaver Coulee.

Theodor lay in his house listening out into the winter night. He saw one of the spruce tree's tops end in a longish lump and knew it was the horned owl. He had been looking at it for half an hour when for the first time it howled out its laughter. The wild sound of laughter remained hanging over coulee and prairie. Now it was night in earnest. Then the coyotes gave an answer, hideous cracked bell sounds, continuing with a varied howling to end with slurping yells as from a creature accursed with its jaws full of blood. When they ceased, the owl answered again. All this kept on for a while, but when the owl screamed for the last time, the coyotes were on the move and didn't respond.

With wild eyes Theodor looked out between the slats. A memory had lodged itself in his mind: Several nights ago an animal had spoken out there which he had never heard before. That voice had silenced everything else alive. It had been everything in one, the night itself with all its devilry. If only it would never come again. When it was silent a painful sigh had come into his heart, a longing for Denmark, for rainy days when because of the weather one was shut in far out in the country. This land shook him, this nightly, insatiable cacophony of coyote howls toward the sky, where the white fire of the northern lights answered back. Winter was hopelessly long. It could certainly never become spring again. Never could the land break out of its straightjacket of ice and snow...

When Charles came over for a visit, Theodor had related to him what he had heard that night. The Metis' eyes sparkled. He hurried outside. Shortly

70

afterward he came back. "It's the lynx you've heard, Theodor. Its tracks are out in the valley. Don't you know the lynx? Don't you have it in Denmark either? I'll try to get it, but the lynx is a roamer, and even if I get it, it can take a long time..."

Theodor lay thinking about the lynx, a large cat with tufts on its ears, Rasmus had said later. The lynx came down from the forests in winter on roaming trips. It screamed horridly, of course, but it wasn't dangerous unless it was wounded...

But Theodor couldn't free himself from the impression it had made on him, and then there was its name. Lynx - link - he put all imaginable terror into that name, and he remembered the lynx's minute-long, trembling wails which could fall off to a soft sound as when the wind whispers through a keyhole - and climb again to a glowing tone which struck him with bodily pain as if needles were being shot into the thirty-two roots of his teeth. A long, piercing whistling note exploded into a crater of sound that swelled beyond all reason. It couldn't be native to the earth; such a performance was created in Hell.

Theodor didn't feel any better. If he were going to die anyway, then why live through the underworld first? His spirits sank. It was not at all easy to be a human being. Whenever he coughed, the cold struck like an icy, slippery body down into his throat, but when it rose up it had tearing barbs. Could Rasmus have been wrong? But it was a shame to ask him, thought Theodor - when it was day. For no night passed without his thinking: "Tomorrow I'll ask."

- - -

He never asked. The days became weeks and months. He lived and suffered. The frost took a little finger and one of his earlobes. But life burned constantly with a pale flickering flame. He almost wanted to die now, but didn't really have the heart for Rasmus's sake to wish to.

12.

Rasmus thought Pedersen should be enlightened about muskrats. Pedersen perked up his ears - almost a dollar for each skin of such miserable rats? - and there were many of them. He and Frederik started making traps on a large scale. They also got interested in hunting coyotes, for Rasmus had already been paying shameful tribute to the coyotes that tore up the traps and nibbled at the rats. They tore a little at the skins but as a rule let them lie. It seemed that even the devil's personal chefs didn't like musk.

Charles became thoughtful when he heard about the coyotes' behavior: Nicoline must have taught them that. Coyotes are much too suspicious to fiddle with a trap. And Rasmus was not more kindly disposed toward Nicoline. She was working more secretly since he had shot off her tail, but her tracks renewed themselves in the valleys after each snowfall. She was both alive and active, though she had relinquished her observation post up on the prairie. Wasn't it Jensen who had wanted Nicoline shot this summer? Indeed, Jensen had been right, and Rasmus became even more furious at Nicoline who, in addition to other malice, had also arranged matters so that Jensen could triumph over him. Beware, Nicoline! But he said it without emphasis, for so far it almost seemed that it was he who should be on his guard against Nicoline.

- - -

One day toward evening Jensen lay thinking about his marriage. By mistake he had fallen asleep in the morning and had been dreaming about Eva. She was obstinate, but since dreams are to be interpreted in the opposite way, he woke up feeling good, though a little disgruntled all the same, for now as likely as not he wouldn't be able to sleep at night.

Just then someone whined at his door. What was it? Jensen didn't want to get out of his box, but since the whimpering continued close to the door he reached for some clothes and got on his feet. He felt so light and bright in his head, so kindly disposed. A long confinement to one's bed makes one sweet-tempered.

He peered out. It was Nicoline. Jensen got quite a fright, but Nicoline was mincing around at a fair distance looking abject. She lay down with her legs in the air and hung her tongue out as if desirous of something. And Jensen suddenly became indignant. That wretch Rasmus had chased that poor animal into distress and misery, and of course he was the one who had cut the tail off the innocent creature! He whistled. "Just come here now, little doggie, here's some rabbit bones for you, poor animal!"

Nicoline began circling, at first rather distant, but then coming forward as she took courage. Jensen tried coaxing her, sat down in his bed and left the door open. Nicoline came near and wriggled her haunches, smiled and let her spittle dribble. After a lot of fuss she came in, shy but lively in every muscle. "There, there, little Nicoline, just come and eat. That Rasmus is a bad lot."

The dog gave a start when he mentioned the name. She looked hard at him for a while, then wriggled her haunches slowly and began to eat. Afterward she wriggled again, walked around herself and grinned lovingly at Jensen. Then she left.

The next day toward evening she was there again, as Jensen had expected. This time she didn't make much fuss. Jensen talked to her, and Nicoline grinned in a friendly way while she ate. "Yes, that Rasmus is a no-good." Nicoline looked toward him, became self-confident in her glance. "Yes indeed, that much we're agreed on," declared Jensen, and Nicoline wriggled her rump.

Each day Nicoline came back, and Jensen began closing the door after her. Nicoline was such good company. Jensen sat on his bed and looked out of the corner of his eye at Nicoline, who sat by the door and looked out of the corner of her eye at him. "That Rasmus is a bad lot," said Jensen with conviction. And Nicoline wrote, yes, on the floor with the slaver from her blue and red chops.

- - -

Charles instructed Rasmus in the treatment of pelts, and Rasmus was a good student. Though his hands were deformed by toil and resembled a kind of working tool, he easily took up things which had to be done. He gnawed indefatigably at the pelts for lack of any better device and didn't think about what illnesses he might contract. Charles while supplying instructions brought up the subject of Jensen, but that topic didn't interest Rasmus. He struck a match on the rear of his trousers, thrust the smoking torch into the bowl of his pipe and said, "Jensen? That skunk! But look, now how about this - is this right, Charley? I'll be a top-notch tanner sometime. Then I'll go to a town and open up a shop, though, heh, you know it would almost be a pity to leave Jensen and sunny Alberta!"

In the middle of his work Charles looked up. "Have you seen anything of Nicoline?"

Rasmus shook his head. "Seen, seen? Her footprints are all over."

"You should try tracking her again. Perhaps she's become more calm now."

They didn't talk any more about it, but the next morning Rasmus rode out with his rifle. Up on the prairie he soon found Nicoline's trail and followed it for a while in long, straight tracks over the plain and through the side valleys. Then it went for a long stretch through the main valley, up over the slopes again, around in an arc on the prairie. Then Rasmus stopped his horse. Here Nicoline had walked many, many times. And the tracks led through a little valley down to Jensen's house. Slowly he rode closer. Here the tracks were thick. And Nicoline must have had her daily walk around the house, if she hadn't even run around here last night just for the fun of it. No, there was a bit of snow in some of the footprints. Rasmus wrinkled his brow and thought. He didn't want to talk with Jensen. But this was strange. He turned his horse into another valley and came back up a little later in front of the house. He straightened himself in the saddle and saw that right up to the door the snow was completely trampled down by dog tracks. A coyote didn't go to people's doors like that.

But Rasmus saw more. Had Jensen become an artist? Two large figures had been painted in black on his door: a man and a dog. Rasmus chewed his plug energetically. Jensen had not drawn that, and he didn't know that it was there, either. Not because Jensen's pure thoughts would prevent it, but because - even if he were an artist, which he wasn't - he would never get the odd idea of decorating his door in that way. Rasmus turned his plug once more and said solemnly, "That painting was done by my fine friend Charles Villeneuve."

He backed his horse a little, turned and rode down into the coulee. He looked back continually. If Nicoline came there by the light of day, she'd not get away alive. And if Jensen got it too...well.

Far over on the other coulee slope Rasmus tethered his horse and waited in a grove of trees. A few hours passed before anything happened. Then the door opened over at Jensen's, and at the same moment Nicoline slunk around the corner of the house and inside. The door closed immediately.

Rasmus jumped onto his horse and rode over the valley with his eyes fixed on the house. Well, so those two had made a conspiracy! Well, Jensen could be handled. But if he were in collusion with Nicoline, then the matter became serious...

Once more Rasmus tethered his horse, waded through the snow higher up and lay down in a bush. His eyes didn't budge from the door. He emptied his rifle of cartridges, cut the points off the lead and reloaded. "Don't expect any mercy, Nicoline. It was bad enough as long as you just kept to four-legged coyotes."

It was growing dark when the door opened. "Goodbye, little Nicoline," sounded Jensen's voice. Yes, goodbye, thought Rasmus, and took aim. Nicoline wasn't standing a foot away from Jensen when Rasmus fired. The stump of lead tore the dog in two. Blood and a rain of chips showered over Jensen, who gave a cry of distress and fell backward in the doorway.

Rasmus got up. He crushed the stumps of Nicoline with two more shots. Then he stared a moment at the slammed door and left.

- - -

The next morning Jensen came out and looked at the remains of Nicoline. That rotten Rasmus!

Then he happened to look at the door, and his knees began to shake under him. He put a finger in the paint. It was easy to remove. Quickly he swept the drawing away with snow.

Afterward Jensen went in, crept into his bed and cried. It was as if the crying came from a child who has suffered injury; he didn't talk to himself as he usually did, he just cried. In the meantime Charles came by. He listened. Wonderment came over his features. He hesitated.

Then he patted his horse lightly and rode on through the coulee. He thought about the shattered Nicoline and understood what had happened. Now Rasmus had quenched his thirst so that presumably *he* at any rate was satisfied. Nicoline would gradually have corrupted the coyotes both in mind and skin, so Charles could be satisfied too.

The next day Jensen came over to Pedersen's. When he noticed that Pedersen wasn't aware of what had happened he became more calm. Could he borrow a horse to ride to town on? It was about time for him to get horses and machines ordered.

Astonished, Pedersen looked at him and readily loaned him a horse. But he never forgave himself that recklessness. Neither the horse nor Jensen appeared afterward in Beaver Coulee. "I'll go fifty-fifty with you on the horse," Rasmus said generously, "for it was money spent for the common good."

"Heh, that Jensen!" said Pedersen and stroked his beard.

- - -

It was as if Nicoline's death had frightened the coyotes. They howled less, began leading a more peripheral existence and familiarized themselves with the thought that Beaver Coulee had been lost to civilization. It had naturally been an advantage when one could yelp down in the valleys where the echo was so marvelous. On the other hand it could be heard farther away up here on the plains where the moon was also more worthy of adulation. They gradually forgot that the coulee had been theirs. And several coy husky-maidens from last year's harvest were so delightful. In spite of everything there was progress in the world.

13.

But miracles could happen! Spring came anyway. Rasmus woke up one night and had to throw the haysack off the blankets - had he absent-mindedly put extra wood on the fire before bedtime? He fell back asleep but woke up anew. He was so strangely happy. Could you be thinking about me, Eva? He dozed a bit again, woke back up and laughed in an undertone. Have I overslept a day since I'm so thoroughly rested? But again he dozed.

Over in his house Theodor lay awake. There were no bad sounds last night at all. And he didn't know how it was, but he expected to hear the singing of birds. The sky was not so strange last night, it was homelike and misty with stars.

Other sounds came that night, but they were gentle, a trembling, greedy tone, deeper than the house-cat's purring, and afterward a subdued chattering. It was the rabbits wiggling their ears and murmuring. Their poor, small hearts had become so hot.

In his bed lay Pedersen, slowly stroking his beard with both hands. Pedersen was old, he knew what had happened, he knew it before he opened his eyes. He looked up in the darkness where he saw a vision, a harrow going over the prairie. And then he and Frederik appeared, with bags hanging around their necks. They were sowing grain...

And Pedersen thought about his wife who lay buried in Montreal.

Everyone came out early that morning to see the goddess of spring walk through Alberta. The melt water streamed down the slopes while the sun danced on the sky. By midday clouds gathered from the southwest. A half hour later it was raining. The lukewarm rain beat down the snow. The coulee became gray. In its bottom the water blustered under the ice. The next day the brook burst its carapace and became a waltzing river. One more day and the river was a flood, the water thundered past some twenty feet from the door of Rasmus' house. A new day and a miracle had occurred: the flood had already fallen off,

79

but right in the extension of Rasmus's house stood Jensen's. It had tried its hand at the role of Noah's Ark and given itself as abandoned goods to Rasmus. Ha, if only Jensen knew! laughed Rasmus. But Pedersen became angry. He had already made preparations to annex the house, and then it sailed, God help us, down to Rasmus...

Rasmus was happy. He needed more space, he felt - and here it came. Pedersen tried to butter him up. "You already have more house than anybody else, so you could very well let me drag off Jensen's palace."

But Rasmus was only amused. No, no, he had more use for a house than just that, and now heaven had decided the matter. The house would not be handed over to anyone but Jensen. "But anyway the fellow would have done better to give us money, Pedersen. We won't get far if we don't have a machine to hitch the oxen to. What would you think if we went to town and saw how it is with credit?"

That was naturally the only right thing to do, and they did so. There was no problem with credit. The machine dealer had never sold anything before, so he was prepared. He supposed they would be dragging others along after them and making a colony of their countrymen out there? "Yes, that's the idea," said Rasmus and slapped Pedersen on the back. "We're writing to the farmers in the old country that here the earth is like butter. Some are very likely already coming this summer, I think."

Then the merchant wrote a letter to the factory about this promising new sphere of interest: The farmers out here were of course still poor, however, so in the beginning they ought to be given both easier credit and lower prices. The factory said yes, and so the man was happy; he tightened up the credit and multiplied the prices by two.

While the harrowing was going on in Beaver Coulee, the Galician Fyodor Murazezsky arrived and put a house on Jensen's homestead. He and his wife were fairly young people with a flock of children that nobody could keep track of. Children were bred out of Murazezsky's hill slopes. Relations became chilly between him and the Danes. He laid claim to Jensen's house and for a short time was undoubtedly considering taking it by force. But Rasmus patted his rifle and said, "Clear out, Fyodor! The house belongs to the user according to the law in these lands. Jensen can have it." Fyodor ground his teeth. But Charles came out of Rasmus's door and looked at the Galician, and the giant made him cautious. His rifle hung on Charles like a fifth limb with veins and nerves in it. Jensen's house remained where it was.

Fyodor plowed with a swarm of half-wild ponies. His wife followed along behind with a similar team hitched to the harrow. In the plow furrows the children ran like a flock of starlings.

80

Rasmus was listening. It was farming with a vengeance. At three o'clock in the morning a yell arose on Fyodor's land. The man roared at the horses and his wife, his wife at the children who were rolling down the hills fighting with each other while the parents toiled the whole day long until it was nine or ten o'clock. What was the idea? thought Rasmus. That Fyodor would certainly set records. But not in Beaver Coulee! Rasmus began to break new land again.

One day he stopped the plow and looked back. He couldn't see the limits of his fields. That would have to be enough for this year. He brushed the sweat from his brow and looked toward the sun which was high and scorching - now he'd harrow and put the last seed in the ground.

When that was done, he started on a trip with a packhorse behind him. Pedersen promised to look after his property. He was curious - but Rasmus was just going away on a slightly longer journey than usual, now that it was spring and on the point of becoming summer.

- - -

And Rasmus rode the long way back to the east through Alberta. He re-experienced everything, but with a longing in his heart - and an anxiety. In reverse order he came through the same regions, luxuriant prairie where the wild rose built lattice-houses and the gopher ran. He rode nights and days through the land of death, he philosophized by the gravestone and tracked the old farm's site. The sun hung burning mercilessly in the sky. Now it was summer in Alberta. And he wasn't going to live in the land of death, but in that of life. In Beaver Coulee...

He camped in the middle of the open prairie at night. A slender column of smoke twisted up where he prepared his food. Then he carefully tramped out the fire, poured water on the ashes and lay down to sleep while the horses walked around whinnying or rolled in the grass with a hollow splashing in their entrails. The days were hot. A thunder shower cooled things down, but again the sun burned over the landscape. Now it was the summer which would last an eternity...

It was the middle of the night when he reached the ranch where Eva was, and he made a halt nearby until daylight.

Eva was walking between the houses when he came and stopped when she saw him. She was as self-assured as before.

"I'm late," he said and jumped off his horse.

"Yes," she said, "for now it's summer."

His heart beat strongly.

"You know well, Eva, why I wanted to come back."

She didn't answer.

"If I'm mistaken," he kept on, trembling, "then I don't want to go in. I'll turn around right now and ride back west."

She looked brightly at him.

"You're not mistaken," she said softly.

They stood silent before each other. Rasmus felt himself in chains.

"It's like this," he said hesitantly. "I can't stay away for very long..."

He looked cautiously at her. She had some words on the tip of her tongue, but waited a bit to say anything.

"I have nothing to wait for, Ross Dane. And the minister doesn't either. He's staying on the ranch until this evening. We can leave today."

Rasmus felt dizzy. He lifted his hands as if to steady himself.

For a moment he felt as if he were afraid. And it was *he* who said,

"It's so sudden."

But neither of them laughed at that. They remained standing and took possession of each other with their eyes until people came and disturbed them.

- - -

Toward afternoon Eva Kristensen Dane rode west from the ranch with her husband. They didn't speak with each other at all. But Rasmus looked at her and thought about the time that had passed since he had seen her last. In the beginning out in Beaver Coulee the longing for her had not been really conscious because so many new things had occupied his mind - but later...it hadn't exactly been *Eva* right away but all aspects of female humanity. An image had fastened itself in his memory from that time - a composite. That vision had come alive again today. But later she had stepped forward distinctly from his background of fantasies, had stepped out of a web of conceptions until she stood large and close by. The time until he could go to her had appeared unreasonable and hopelessly long.

- - -

Now he rode here by her side on a mild, hazy day which reminded him of his childhood in Denmark. And if it were necessary this woman could under-stand his childhood language even though she didn't speak it yet. She was descended from Danes and Norwegians.

His thoughts travelled far. Who was she actually, *what* was she? - this was indeed like a lottery! He looked affectionately at her - at any rate an attractive lottery. What he had just done counted for all days, it counted until death parted them, it was a serious matter. Wasn't this the first time he had embarked on something which couldn't just be dropped whenever it suited him? Now he was truly entrusted to fate, wonderfully entrusted! And so was Eva - she most of all.

- - -

By the time the sun was setting they had left the Youngstown district. Hesitatingly Rasmus pulled up his horse. It was probably best to have something to eat...

He made a fire, and she cooked while he looked after the animals. Then they sat across from each other and ate, talking about the surroundings - and about the moon which was sailing up into the air, large and fiery red over a grove of poplars far off. The coyote gave its gentle summer-night yelp, and the rabbits slipped in and out with their kind eyes.

Rasmus's back hurt a bit from sitting. Eva's must certainly hurt also, but what...

Eventually he got up and stretched his limbs. She did the same. Rasmus fiddled with a saddle. He didn't look at Eva. Then she went resolutely over to him and whispered, "Ross, you haven't even kissed your wife yet."

Moved, he turned around and grasped her. She pressed herself to him and laughed a little, but became silent when he lifted her up violently. He looked around keenly and irresolutely, walking first a bit one way then another as if they were hunting and had to hide. When he was about to change direction the third time, he stopped as if composed and looked down at her closed eyes.

In the tall grass under the moon they celebrated their wedding night, while the coyote's broken bell sounded on the prairie.

Late at night when the moon had made the trip over into another part of the sky, Rasmus sat up and looked around. The prairie lay white, full of elfin maids. Eva's mouth had become very large and pale.

14.

Eva and Rasmus didn't come home to peace in Beaver Coulee. When Rasmus pulled up his horse on the prairie over the valleys, he saw that Jensen's house was gone. His eyes narrowed. His glance went over to Pedersen's farm. It wasn't there. He rode over a couple of rises and saw that the house was at Fyodor's. So that's the way it is. The Galician wants war. Then he'll get it.

They rode down to Pedersen's. He was embarrassed. "Well, all is not well here as you can probably see," he said and cast a sidelong glance at Eva. Rasmus had got himself a wife!

"You promised to look after my property," said Rasmus sharply.

"What was I supposed to do?" said Pedersen. "Fyodor took the house during the night. He had gone quite a way with it by the time we got up. No, no, I didn't mix myself up in it at all - there could have been shooting. I only had Frederik..."

"Now I want to see how you live," said Eva. "Then I'm sure we'll get that house back from the Galician."

Rasmus nodded.

"Well," he said to Pedersen, laughing and somewhat mollified, "if I'd been alone perhaps Fyodor could have tricked me. But now - no way!"

And he rode home with Eva.

She looked around the house and immediately set to work. Imperceptibly everything changed appearance. Just small changes made it different.

"We'll make it nice," she said confidently. "And before winter you should build a shelter of logs to the north and east. When do you want to get your house at Fyodor's?"

"Tomorrow."

"You can't do it alone, for they won't leave you alone to do it. I'm coming along."

"Never."

But Eva rumpled his hair. Of course she was coming along. And Rasmus

85

yielded, but she'd certainly regret it...

Rasmus lay in bed looking at Eva, who was standing in the brightest part of the room fixing her hair for the night. It was thick and long and as she stood there in the half-light, he began thinking of pretty pictures he had seen. There was one in particular which had been in an illustrated Bible they had had down in South Dakota. It represented Eve standing naked with long hair among green trees. Later his father had used pen and ink to provide her with a long dress and puff sleeves, for such a picture would only put ideas into young people's heads and should never have been printed in a Bible. Rasmus had only thought it was pretty and didn't understand that *that* could be called ideas in the head. Now he suddenly began to think that it must have been his moralizing father who as a matter of course had imbued others with his own feelings.

He followed Eva with his eyes. Now he had truly a reason for being in Alberta. He saw, as if from a bird's eye view, a long succession of golden years. His heart became full: Eva, Eva.

When she had gone to bed she put her hands under her head and said, almost more to the room than to him, "You know you're the only one. Never do anything, Ross, to make me...go my way."

"What would that be?"

He was almost afraid.

"That you even only once preferred someone else."

He laughed and took her into his arms.

"I am Ross Dane," he said and thought that was enough. "Now you must take note of what you dream the first night here. It means a lot, you know."

- - -

Eva dreamed that night that her husband was standing up on the highest hill by Beaver Coulee with a church behind him. Billowing fields lay round about for miles. The prairie lark twittered from the hillocks. But the brook at the bottom of the valley was full of knives.

- - -

The next morning Pedersen saw Rasmus driving his oxen up toward Fyodor's homestead. Pedersen opened his eyes wide. Eva had come along in men's clothing, carrying a shotgun. Rasmus himself had his rifle over his shoulder. "Oh, well, now peace is at an end - in sunny Alberta!" He kept himself indoors with Frederik. You could get yourself mixed up in enough rows!

No one came out from the farm. Since the door of Jensen's house was closed,

Rasmus forced it open and began throwing various pieces of junk outside. As if by magic the whole Murazezsky family appeared, twenty sparkling eyes - and a raging flood of abuse in a language which Rasmus and Eva didn't understand. Then Fyodor finally switched into his clumsy English. "You yourself say house belongs to user!" he screamed. "Get you off my homestead, or else - kra - kra - kra..."

Rasmus's body gave a start. Tobacco juice began seeping out of the corners of his mouth.

"Yes," he said hoarsely. "And now *I'm* using it. Get away!"

Eva drove closer with the oxen. Fyodor threw a word over to her. She opened her eyes wide for a second but didn't stop.

But that word hit home in Rasmus. He wanted to control himself, but his feet almost became elastic, and the ground rocked. He let his chin sink, chewed his plug convulsively and approached Fyodor, who made himself tall and said, "Swede monkeys come here to steal peaceful man's house!"

That didn't make it any better. Monkey, never mind. But Swede! Rasmus had known only one Swede, a real skunk, a thief...

He jumped on Fyodor. A howl arose from all the Murazezskys, so Pedersen and Frederik pressed their noses hard against the window pane. His wife lashed at Rasmus from behind with a rope. All the little Murazezskys ran around in an orgy of yelling. Eva acted calmly. She let the oxen stand, bent down so that no one saw her and sent a burst of shot straight up in the air. Mrs. Murazezsky gave out a whine and ran from the men, wailing and chasing the children inside. "Murder! Murder! Murder!"

The eyes of Frederik and his father met. They knew each other at that moment.

"Now they're shooting," said Pedersen quietly.

Fyodor twisted like a viper. He gave Rasmus a knee in the abdomen, bit into his throat. Nicoline! thought Rasmus and tightened his hands around Fyodor harder until the Galician with a sigh let his head fall down on his shoulder and passed out.

Rasmus looked for a moment at the man's face, chalk white against his dark hair. "Have you been tamed then, Murahusky? Next time you'll please remember that we don't run off with other people's houses here in sunny Alberta!"

They laid the man in the grass and hitched the oxen to the house. Rasmus stood up on the roof and directed, while Eva brought up the rear with the shotgun. No attempt was made to stop them.

"You see, Frederik," lectured Pedersen, "that's a dirty business. Such a house isn't worth all that when you have enough material for another one. It got damaged by sailing down to Rasmus's and even worse by being hauled up to Fyodor's. Now it will probably fall apart completely. No, don't look for a quarrel unless there's money at stake."

- - -

Charles came riding along and heard about the war. He nodded. That sort of thing should be stifled right at the start. He looked from Eva to Rasmus and thought that everything was pretty good.

"It looks, though, as if Theodor is better," he said suddenly - as if it were something evil.

"Well?" said Rasmus questioningly and looked at him. "Isn't that good?"

Charles looked him straight in the eye.

"No," he said. "Whatever Death has marked he will keep a grip on, even if it has tricked him."

Rasmus didn't like Charles's saying such a thing. When he had gone, Rasmus shuffled around a bit. Then he said,

"Oh, rubbish, that's just an injun belief. That sort of thing doesn't mean anything any more."

- - -

Eva revealed herself as a woman who was well-off. She had a couple of hundred dollars, a fantastic sum which she handed over to Rasmus without stipulations. He thought it over for a couple of hours, then rode to town and ordered wood. The next morning he leveled ground higher up in the coulee where he could see that the water had never been. He sweated over the shovel and spat far. Now there'd be a house!

Pedersen got his shovel and set to work as well. He didn't proceed like Rasmus but had a tough persevering way of using his shovel which in the long run was more effective. "Oh, yes indeed, marry a rich woman, that's the way to do it," he laughed. "There won't be anything but an injun for me though. And that's no good even if the redmen are very decent. So damned many children come out of an injun, and you get too old just when they're most expensive to have. And don't you get feeling like a hen seeing its nest full of ducklings?"

Rasmus sent a whole clothesline of spit over his building site. His glance was distant. "That'll be four feet," he said, meditating, "and then I need some big granite boulders."

"No, I guess I'd better just stay as I am," Pedersen went on. "The other is too risky."

"Not when you have a strong iron hook," mumbled Rasmus.

"What?" said Pedersen.

Rasmus looked up. "What?" he said.

Then they got back to it with their shovels.

"Heh, that Jensen," said Pedersen for no apparent reason.

"Well, now we can see that he's raised devils on his homestead," said Rasmus. "Seven times eight is, what is that? And minus six then is fifty. With a bar on top. I want to buy one of those lamps on a sliding bar. That's something really nice."

- - -

Wood came, and Rasmus built. He never took a rest, and the sun never saw him in bed. He hammered, sawed and did carpentry work the whole day, danced round like a squirrel, balanced on the scaffolding, hovered in mid-air with a board as if he wanted to go flying. He hung in or out of a window, beat his fingers blue and got furious about nails that disappeared. Eva stood quietly and listened many times a day. She knew the whole thing was for her glory. And the other day she had been able to confide something to him which made him shorten the night by two hours more...

15.

Theodor sat in his bed listening to the distant hammering over at Rasmus's. They were at work out there. Here he sat. Indeed, he was better, but never happy, and he still had to hold out one more winter. To think about it was almost too much to bear. They had stopped visiting him, it had become so natural for him to be lying there. He never complained, so why feel pity for him? When he himself thought he had it good, the others could also be content.

Now that the wheat billowed on the prairie, his father came and moaned: How were they going to get it shipped that long, long way to the railroad? That would mean driving with wagon and sled for an eternity, before they were through. Horrible trips! But Theodor stifled a sigh. If only he could be allowed to haul grain rather than lying here getting months and years cut from his life. "Well, little Theodor, I'm glad things are going well for you. I'm going over to Rasmus's..."

Theodor figured they came only because they thought it would be wrong not to. Except Rasmus - he came so remarkably often since he'd got married, and Eva occasionally brought treats. He ate them greedily, for he was always hungry, and when she had gone, the others of course came to have a taste, if anything were left over. You couldn't object to that, he thought, but they certainly wouldn't have done it if they knew how hungry he always was. Theodor didn't dare really to look at Eva Dane. She was so big and pretty, it was as if the blood ran from her veins over into his whenever she was near him. Whenever she turned her back, his eyes hung bewitched on her. Theodor didn't understand it. Now when he was on the way back to life, life didn't accept him as before. Or had *he* become another person..?

When the heat in the middle of the day was so oppressive that he slid into a torpid state, he would see Eva walking over green meadows. Or she would bend over him and put her cool lips on his forehead. Eva, she noticed nothing. She came several times and was dissatisfied with the way he was lying. Then she took the blankets off him, spread them on the floor and carried him over on to them so that she could make the bed. It cut him in his soul - he was only a sick boy in her eyes, nothing else. But he was in his eighteenth year. Her strong, superior treatment made him shudder, but he longed for it anyway. Eva, she noticed nothing.

- - -

A caravan came through the valley. Fyodor was with it; therefore nobody went down to see the strangers. Rasmus followed them with dagger-like eyes from the roof of his house: a new collection of Galicians. It was definitely time to do something about what he had made the machine dealer believe - Scandinavians must be brought to Beaver Coulee. Rasmus's new dog - it was called Jack, for Rasmus wasn't going to have another Nicoline affair - stood growling. Jack always accepted his master's views. He hated Fyodor and all his clan.

Rasmus went in and talked with Eva. The Galicians were growing too numerous! There were both Norwegians and Danes down in the States he could write to - but it was frankly more difficult for him to write a letter than to build a dozen houses. She could get the names and write to them. She set about doing that right away, and Rasmus crawled up onto his house again, filled with awe at Eva's handwriting. She was a model wife, and the farm was going to be a model farm - ow, damn it, my thumb! - but it wasn't going to lie in the middle of a Galician colony - not his farm.

He also asked Pedersen to write to acquaintances, but of course they lived way off in Denmark, said Pedersen, and besides he thought that there might be enough people here with those who came of their own accord. Whether they were Galicians or Chinese he felt didn't make any difference.

"Well, so that's what you think," Rasmus spat and went on. "I've certainly noticed that there was a bit of Galician in you from the time you let the husky over there drag off my house. All the more use there is for whites here."

Pedersen looked after him and stroked his beard. Danes or Galicians, wasn't it all the same? Here money should be made, not kingdoms, it seemed to him. Heh, whether Rasmus called him one thing or another, the sun shone equally as radiantly over - sunny Alberta!

- - -

One morning the harvester began rattling on Rasmus's homestead. Pedersen listened and looked, then afterward took a walk into the almost man-high wheat. One should actually wait the better part of a week yet, he thought, but Rasmus of course knew the land. It was a pitiful sight to see all those weeds, roses and muck in the grain, but it could be cut off fairly high since the straw was just going to be burned off. Better get down to it right away.

And in the afternoon the harvester was going at Pedersen's. The next morning its great wheel was also turning over Fyodor's wheat. At the new colonist's, who had taken a homestead near the coulee opposite Fyodor, they were toiling with house building. Theodor lay listening to the whole thing while Eva ran outside playing with his little sisters, who were shouting with joy at her stunts. "Now goodbye, kids. I'm going over to work in the field."

His temper darkened when he heard her running. She'd been in man's clothes today. It had given him quite a jolt when he saw that. Now he couldn't forget it.

He listened to the harvester's rattling which rose and fell according to the direction of the wind, or as it moved closer or farther away. He pictured Eva following the harvester, saw her handling the sheaves. And he felt a bitterness toward Rasmus because he was sitting on the machine, seeing her the whole time and saying whatever he wanted to.

- - -

One evening the new man came up to Rasmus's. He remained standing inside the door calmly scrutinizing him and Eva. He was thickset, with low and broad forehead. His beard grew densely on his face.

"I've taken a homestead here in Beaver Coulee, and my name is Ivan," he said. "I wanted to say hello to my neighbours."

Until now Rasmus had sat looking stiffly at the man. Now he got up and gave him his hand.

"Welcome, Ivan, and I hope we'll be getting along better together with you than with your countryman."

Ivan looked him straight in the eyes the whole time, alert but not unfriendly.

"Fyodor has told me a story," he said. "At first I didn't doubt it was true, for you Scandinavians are often somewhat haughty fellows. But my daughter - I have nearly grown children - was taking a walk yesterday evening alone in the coulee - well, nothing happened...beyond my cracking one of Fyodor's ribs."

Rasmus thought a little bit about that.

"That sounds strange. Fyodor has been driving his harvester all day."

"Yes, I know. He's a hard man. I'm sorry about this, for blood of course is thicker than water anyway. But whatever kinds of people come here to this district - I hope for neighbourliness with all of them."

Rasmus switched over to Danish, "What do you think, Eva, if we give Ivan

93

that house Fyodor took? We don't have much use for it. It would look good. Then it would show that it wasn't for the sake of the house that we took it from Fyodor."

"Yes," she said.

He turned to Ivan. "We took that house from Fyodor because he stole it while no one was here. You'll want to start plowing - you can take the house if you like."

Ivan was overjoyed. He took a couple of steps forward and scarcely knew what to say.

"But guard against giving it to Fyodor," said Eva, and gave him a meaningful look.

Ivan laughed. "Then I'll see about getting my house home!"

- - -

Pedersen became furious at Rasmus. "Didn't you come here calling me a Galician because I wasn't so fond of Danes as you? You're a nice countryman. I asked you for the house when I could have used it, the time it was just as much mine as yours. And now you make a present of it to a Galician..."

"In the first place I'll tell you," said Rasmus coolly, "that at that time I also had use for the house. And if you yourself don't see the difference between Galicians and Danes, you can't expect others to. Thirdly, I'm conducting high politics while you're an ass with a long beard. You could have built twenty of that kind of house this summer instead of running around fondling wheat ears!"

- - -

Almost all the grain was stooked on the prairie when Fyodor came over to Pedersen's one evening. He didn't look any of them in the eye.

Fyodor was bitter. He spoke derogatorily about this damned land where no one had justice done to him, and everything was so backward. Like most of the Galicians he spoke poor English; the language was too foreign to their tongues. But Fyodor had taught himself the expletives to excess. These he knew well and had even composed more. One saw in his eyes that profanity was also his natural form of expression. Fyodor had black, sparkling eyes and never blinked. Whatever his look touched on turned cold. He thought moreover that Pedersen and he had something to talk about. Now that the threshing faced them, what sense was there in those two Danes' renting a threshing machine jointly, as they had done, and excluding him? Did they have money like grass, maybe? It was better to pay only a third than a half.

94

Pedersen agreed with him. "But what can I say, Fyodor? Ross doesn't want to. I told Ross that, but he said that I could just rent jointly with you if I wanted to. Then *he'd* go it alone. And of course you know very well, Fyodor Murazezsky, that here in Beaver Coulee it pays to sing the same tune as Ross Dane..."

Fyodor got up. Yes, he saw that, but he dared say it would be different some time. Anyway Pedersen should try to talk with Ross one more time...

Pedersen looked up abruptly. "Yes," he said. "You can look in again later."

And Pedersen went over to Rasmus's, who became irritated when he heard what his errand was. Hadn't they talked enough about that matter? Pedersen could undo the lease if he wanted and ally himself with Fyodor. No one was stopping him.

Pedersen was silent for a while.

"I don't see why we absolutely have to have war and lose money here," he said slowly. "None of us are rich. And you can think what you want to about Galicians..."

"I don't think anything about Galicians," Rasmus interrupted, "but I think a whole lot about Fyodor."

"You can also think what you want to about him - just let him be a scoundrel. But he has many small children, they've been hungry this summer, he's run into debt - now winter is around the corner, and you want to chase him off his homestead. I don't want to talk about your conscience, but you know Fyodor is crazy..."

Rasmus sat looking at Pedersen, who seemed to grow larger. "And what I want to say to you is that if you don't change your mind then you'll be alone, and I'll go to the Galicians!"

Rasmus looked Pedersen derisively up and down. "What Galicians? You must be forgetting that there aren't any but Fyodor. You'd do better not to take sides with people who want to drive each other out of Beaver Coulee, for it could happen that..."

Pedersen subsided to his natural size. It was true; Ivan no longer belonged with Fyodor. And probably in time it would be mostly Scandinavians who would come here.

Rasmus chewed his plug.

"All right, you can tell your friend Fyodor that we'll include him. But we won't trust him. That's why we'll thresh at his place last. I don't want to starve him out. But remind him from me that he'll never be content here in this district."

- - -

Pedersen had obtained what he wanted and went to Fyodor, who silently listened to his account. "Then we'll thresh jointly," said Fyodor, "but you can tell Ross that one day he'll regret falling afoul of Fyodor!"

Pedersen however found no reason to say anything to Rasmus, for then he'd probably be unco-operative again.

16.

One night Eva lay unable to sleep. She was in a despondent mood; had never felt like this before. She usually slept soundly. Could it be on account of the moon? It shone white into the room. Shadows from the crossbars of the window lay over the floor. She walked slowly from the bed and looked out. In the quiet night no sound could be heard but the irregular tinkling from the belled cow. Jack was carrying on down in the valley with a coyote which was taunting him by constantly keeping the same distance between them, but nipping his hocks each time Jack got tired of the game and turned around. Irritated, Jack would spin around and set off in pursuit of the coyote, which kept its distance with a couple of elegant bounds. Deeply offended, Jack eventually went slowly home, sniffing at bushes and stones with great interest. His tormentor sat on a clump of earth outlined in sharp silhouette. Eva saw it was a husky, more dog than wolf.

As she looked out into the white night she felt a current move through her which she had never experienced before - as if a new cycle had arisen in her body. But she wasn't sick.

In the coulee fall's muted colours had long superseded each other. Now the moonlight made the valleys white. The great nightjar was still in the land, passing intermittently the window as it showed its white wing section. The sky was divided into bands, the lowermost resting coal blue on the prairie. Higher up was a lilac belt, highest a sky-blue one without stars. On the hills the grain stood in stooks, a moon landscape...

Eva sighed, turned away from the windowpane and looked at Rasmus. He lay in a twisted position with his head on his elbow and right hand clenched on the blanket. She tried to recall her familiar feelings for him but suddenly couldn't. They were gone. She looked at him again and shuddered. He was solely a paragon of strength. His fingers were like iron hooks, his lips were curved back, his mouth ready to bite. She believed suddenly she was seeing *man*, all men without a veil of erotic haze, a greedy and living bundle of muscles, man, who took what he wanted and filled the world with pain.

- - -

Her mood from the night had not died down when it became day, but
Rasmus didn't notice. He bolted down his food and went out to the threshing
machine. He had been a bit ill for several days; she saw that now he had a
fever. His face was pale, his forehead sweating, and his eyes were dull. But he
said nothing, took it only as an offence, something that wanted to have it in for
him, but would damned well not succeed. She abhorred him. He reeked of life!

Disheartened, she walked later in the morning up onto the prairie. The sky
was clear, but the wind blew cold. She wanted to be alone, not to risk anyone's
coming to talk. In a grove of poplars she found a cozy place where the sun was
shining. There she hid deep in the growth. A slender little spider accepted her
right away as an eternal thing and stretched its net between her shoes. There
in the weak reflection of summer she noticed how the insects died and the earth
fell asleep. Now it was time to rest and gather strength for a new summer. The
sun went behind a cloud no larger than itself, but immediately it was as if the
shadow whispered in her face: "Now November's coming, now winter's
coming."

Each time she made a slight movement something happened near her - an
animal withdrew quickly in the grass or a bird flew off. Far and near the crows'
rasping fall voices sounded. A squirrel came running, caught sight of her and
beat a retreat up into a tree, informing anyone who cared to listen by its loud
chattering that here was something overwhelming and awful. Eva gave a start
at the sound. Then it grew dark before her eyes. She reached out moaning,
and the squirrel howled even more loudly. Slowly she gained control over
herself again, gradually becoming completely calm. Dread fought with joy. It
was so brutal. The little thing, it would very likely become a new Ross Dane!
And she remembered Ross, tears springing to her eyes. She had to be careful
what she was thinking and doing while this was going on.

- - -

When Rasmus was on the way home in the evening, she was waiting for him
on one of the hills. It looked like bad weather. Out in the west a rainbow formed,
in front of it another and again another as if a barrel vault were being built over
toward the sunset. The low prairie hills were gilded by the sun, and under the
wild thundering heavens blackbirds flew like sparks of fire. A stud of horses
blustered through the rainbow vault toward the farm.

Several times they had fought against fire in the valleys. Fields burnt black lay here and there. It was as if a spirit had stretched its finger down and written on the ground.

Leaning against each other, Rasmus and Eva walked above the coulee as the horse followed along and in a friendly way nudged their backs with its muzzle.

- - -

It was late before the threshing began on Fyodor's land, but they worked hard. Before it grew light each raw morning, they got started while the wind hurled the half-pulverized straw far and wide. Close by it was like a cloud of smoke, farther away a rain of ashes. The straw tumbled from the blower down over the stack like a mob of trolls cavorting. From dawn to dusk Rasmus was active and made Pedersen and Frederik hurry too, for Fyodor should not have the slightest grounds for saying that they had sabotaged his threshing. Violent storms came, but they kept at it; the smoking jet of straw from the blower shot out a distance of half a mile, but they worked on, no mawkishness! And when the first snow arrived, they were on the way to town with the threshing machine.

Fyodor's ratlike eyes went in circles around Rasmus. He pondered. There was no doubt that he and Rasmus were the fastest people in Beaver Coulee. That house business shouldn't have stood between them. And Ivan, that ass, had blabbed to the sanctimonious Danes about that little episode one evening in the coulee when he had affectionately put his arms around Ivan's daughter's waist - very much to the detriment of his health. Fyodor ground his teeth. That fool Ivan, what did it hurt him if someone cuddled his daughter a little? If *that* hadn't been in the way he could now have been on better terms with Rasmus, who was probably uneasy about his wife. Now Rasmus spoke loud about child molesters whenever Fyodor came close. Fyodor swore softly. Wasn't the girl fourteen? There would come a day when they all would get what was coming to them - first Ivan, that renegade!

17.

They had had a good harvest. And now the month-long transport south began in large, clumsy sleds. The men were seldom at home. The prairie was snowed over, but the sled tracks led south continually from Beaver Coulee. Now they longed for the railway. With frost on face and hands they came home from the week-long trips with dead coyotes in their sleds, were thawed out with hot drinks and put to bed for a day and a night before they loaded and sledded off again.

No one could wait, for no one had any money. And when all the credit was settled, they weren't rich. But they had houses and machines which were theirs. And Rasmus bought pretty things for his wife. He also thrust a bunch of banknotes into her hand. "It's for the doctor, Eva. If it's too little you can have again as much!"

- - -

Pedersen prepared his accounts and was satisfied. But he was a bit afraid. Not a furrow had been plowed. How would it go in the spring? Charles came and comforted him - but you must have at least two or three plows in the ground.

Pedersen sighed. New expenditures, even if one got value back for them. Wealth was certainly not *cash* in this land.

- - -

Theodor became more lonely than ever. He almost never saw his brother. Frederik had shot up. He considered himself grown up while the older Theodor was only a snivelling child no one needed to reckon with. Frederik's resemblance to his father grew continually, and when Rasmus as a result was reminded how Pedersen must have looked as a young boy, his liking for him didn't increase. Frederik chewed a whole pound of tobacco a week; he even dried it and chewed it twice. The lower part of his face was always moving counterclockwise in a revolving motion. His eyes were fearless and audacious. Ivan cracked his whip whenever Frederik sneaked around on his property. But Frederik could work. His father couldn't compare with him. And Frederik was a competent judge of money. In that way Pedersen was well off.

The girls looked after themselves. Young as they were they went to bed, got up, dressed and undressed and ate just as it suited them. They became like a couple of wild flowers. They got what they wanted whenever they could get it themselves, otherwise not. They lived in their own nether region on the farm. No one meddled in their affairs. They were healthy and self-assured, speaking the adults' gruff language to perfection. Pedersen looked at them now and then as if he had never seen them before: "Heh, heh, what might such a pair of fish go and become?" They were away whole days without anyone's thinking about it, catching gophers which they roasted whenever the home food became too monotonous for them. If they came in to see Theodor it was almost accidental. They hardly understood that he was the only one who to the best of his poor ability tried to look after them a bit.

But not even he spent much time thinking about them. He was occupied with his own game of life, which gave him enough to worry about. Throughout the fall he feared winter, almost wearing himself out in dread of it. But when it came he was, of course, right in the middle of it, so it was not so bad. He lay in his bed and knew that he loved Eva Dane. As time went on she gradually came less and less often - and the last time he understood why she wasn't doing so much walking now. It gave him some hard weeks. He had to struggle through everything his fantasy ruthlessly made him visualize about her and Rasmus, until that too receded in his consciousness. She kept on living as a dream of his.

He improved, got steadily better, but mentally he aged, and his face showed the furrows of a man in his forties. He had run through most of life's gamut without having lived - and had been out in many places that most people wisely stayed away from. There he had learned not to believe in any happiness. He knew there was none.

One day in February, in the dead of winter, Rasmus was strolling around on his land with his rifle, setting the straw stacks on fire. He remained standing for a long time by the last one, looked first at it, then at the other ones which were sending clouds of smoke bulging over the white plains. He thought that the time was not far off when bonfires of straw in the winter would light up the nights in all of Alberta and eastward, as far as the prairie went.

Rasmus became lost in thought while the stack he was standing beside burned down until it became black, and each gust of wind made the black, grooved hill glow. Then he tore himself loose and went homeward. He musn't be away too long at this time.

A distance from the farm he stood still, frightened. Then he began running, jumping like a stag over the drifts. Eva was in labour. Rasmus came running out into the snow again, tied a cloth firmly on the outer wall and ran back in. Five minutes later from the window he saw Frederik driving his horse up over the slope on his way to town. Frederik was not sparing the animal, but Rasmus sank his nails deep into his flesh. Why didn't the boy hurry up?

Pedersen came a little later, but Rasmus drove him out. He couldn't bear to have anyone hearing Eva's screams; he was crazy and shaken by pangs of conscience. Some time later Pedersen came again, but thought Rasmus was going to murder him. Then he went over and spoke to Ivan's wife, but Rasmus spotted her far away and appeared in the door with his rifle. She hurried back home.

It was a night of madness, and when it had passed Eva and Rasmus were not the same people. When the first frenzy had subsided, his brain so to speak closed up. Deaf and blind, he did the right thing without having the slightest idea about it beforehand and without remembering a scrap of it afterward. But Eva's screams would ring in his ears for years afterward, and he had never before this night known how much he loved her. Never more would she go through that hell. He could have gone out into the stable and hanged himself if she hadn't needed his help so badly.

Frederik came riding late at night and knocked on Rasmus's door. In the dark corridor Rasmus came and asked if he had the doctor with him.

"No," said Frederik breathlessly, "he wasn't in town. I tried to find him and later on went to town again, but he wasn't there."

"It doesn't matter any more," snarled Rasmus. "Just ride on home."

At that moment he opened the door into the parlour. In the light from the lamp Frederik saw him a moment and nearly fell off his horse. Rasmus was bloody from top to toe, and madness blazed in his eyes.

- - -

The next morning it was rumoured in Beaver Coulee that Eva Dane had given birth during the night to three vigourous boys.

At first Pedersen was stunned. Then he stroked his beard and laughed. "Heh, heh, pretty damn good soil for growing things - in sunny Alberta!"

Second Part
1.

It was misty. At intervals it drizzled. In the depressions in the slimy ground were puddles, and on the horizon here and there hung the distant smoke from steam threshing machines. Among the many thickets which lay as if blown around on the prairie stood the straw stack's typical shape, steep on the one side which had faced the threshing machine, on the other side evenly slanting. The blown out straw stood like golden mountains on the dark brown stubble fields. Here and there year-old stacks were standing so close to the houses that it would have been dangerous to burn them off - or perhaps they had been left for the sake of the horses and livestock. They were narrower at the root than higher up - like skerries that had been lapped by the waves for a thousand years. Crows flew over the ground, and flights of ducks went by like snakes in the autumn sky where the clouds hung low, curved into each other like corrugated iron. An anticipation of winter was over the land.

Ross Dane sat on his wagon absorbed in thoughts and let the horses look after themselves. They stopped now and then and grazed by the side of the road, whinnied in melancholy sounds and walked on. Ahead stretched the road's blue black, muddy strip, a gaping incision which had been carved through the wild land. If Ross turned around he saw the same thing - a long black road. Where the mowers had dislodged a stone in the cut field, it glistened as if from a dark and dewy eye. Swarms of birds lay in the twig-wreathed ponds. There was constantly a hawk sailing under the sky. From the bogs legions of ducks took off. The rabbit came out on the road, looked around with its bright child eyes and thoughtfully poured the water out of one ear before it occurred to it that there could be danger here and cleared off with its rump in the air.

Good! All was right with the world. It was unnecessary and only a waste of time to philosophize. The main thing was to look after one's own business - and do it well. But Ross had been off in contemplations a while, trying to find a background for what had happened in Beaver Coulee - and what could possibly happen in the future? First there was the fact that Eva thought the boys should go to town to school, later to college. Ross didn't quite dare say anything. He had an enormous respect for learning. But there was now no harm either if the boys learned to work. This business of reading how something should be done and then not being able to do it - that didn't appeal to him. The schoolmaster was like that, and savoury he was not. If one toiled and strove, put all his ability into doing a thing, then the teacher came slinking along and made a note of the mistakes. Ross smiled spitefully, heh, sound profession for a man. Though naturally a rewarding occupation. He wished something better than that for his boys.

Ross struck with the reins, set the horses trotting. He was out to get hold of one more fellow for the threshing and wanted to make use of the opportunity to drop in on a Danish family which already had come a fairly long time ago. No longer of course did you have to ride thirty miles to enjoy the sight of a Dane. Lord knows you didn't. There was trouble enough with those that came on their own. But this was a married man, and perhaps he would like to work for Ross.

A little later he reached the place. There wasn't any farmhouse there - rather, an old transportable grainary. It was ramshackle, and the door couldn't be closed.

A woman came out with several small children hanging on her skirt. With yielding eyes she looked toward the stranger, and Ross saw she was afraid he'd speak a language she didn't understand. It was pitiful to see her standing there in the pouring rain, and the sight burned itself into Ross - this wife of a bankrupt Danish farmer deposited on the desolate prairie in a miserable shed which storm and rain went through. Her eyes showed she had cried her fill.

"Hello", said Ross.

Her eyes lit up.

"Hello", she answered.

"I'm Ross Dane. I've come to ask if your husband wants work."

"He's not home."

"When's he coming?"

"I don't know."

"Does he have work?"

"I don't know."

"When did he leave?"

"Three weeks ago."

Ross looked keenly at her. Then he got off the wagon and followed her in.

"Where did he go?"

"South. There wasn't any work here at the time."

"And you haven't heard from him since?"

"No."

Ross looked around in the room.

"You don't have any food", he said slowly, "and you've been starving."

The woman sat down crying.

"Now we have a little money. Now we'll get some food," she said.

"Has he sent money then?"

"No."

"Have you borrowed?"

"No, two people came here and wanted to do business. So I sold the cows."

Ross took out tobacco and paper, rolled a cigarette and lit it.

"What were their names?"

"It was Pedersen and his son Frederik."

"Oh. And what did they give you for the cows?"

"Eight dollars apiece."

Ross took the cigarette in his hand and looked at her with open mouth.

"Eight dollars? How in the devil's name...."

The woman looked up angrily.

"It's easy enough for you to talk! The children were crying from hunger. From Jens I heard nothing...."

"What is it with him actually?" interrupted Ross. "Does he think you can live off grass?"

"I suppose he imagines that somebody's helping us."

There was an accusation in the words, and Ross lost his temper.

"It's always help, help, help", he hissed. "We old ones here came to Beaver Coulee without any help but ourselves. We didn't taste bread for months. Sometimes we were ready to eat our own excrement. What we have has cost us sweat and years. But now they come running in droves, help me here, help me there, button up my pants. A man leaves his wife and children to themselves in the middle of the prairie, for they will certainly get help! What do people learn in Denmark nowadays? Probably nothing except that hunger is forbidden, and with that learning they travel over here where starving to death is gloriously allowed if that's all one's good for. But your husband will probably learn that. There are also people here who need to learn something, and now I'm going over and visit Pedersen! I'll drag him over the coals so his brain turns around in his skull, that thief."

And Ross went out, jumped into the wagon and thundered off.

By the time he reached Pedersen's farm he had calmed down. Relations had not been good for a long time between Pedersen and Ross Dane. Gossip and quarrelling had split the colony's Danish elements into two sides with Ross and Pedersen as major figures. Ordinarily one behaved as if nothing had happened, but many times the resentment broke out. The older ones sided with Ross, but the newer ones, often dissatisfied and disappointed people, went to Pedersen who spoke so sympathetically and was indignant at Ross' brutal methods.

It was Frederik who received him.

"Well, look here," said Frederik, grinning while his eyes were on guard, "it's a great event to see the king of Beaver Coulee!"

"Is your father home?"

"He's inside. Come in, he'll be happy, you can bet...."

"Heh, heh, hello Ross, how are you?" laughed Pedersen. "Is the wheat good?"

"The wheat's good enough. Be happy if yours is just as good. By the way I hear you've been dealing in cows."

Frederik looked Ross in the eyes. Theodor lifted his head and looked at them. He saw a storm coming.

"Well?" said Frederik teasingly.

"Certainly, heh, heh, that's true enough," declared Pedersen. "Of course we had heard something about Jens's leaving his wife alone, and then we drove over to see if we could help. We did so by buying a couple of cows that she had no use for, yes indeed. You'd probably like coffee?"

Ross ate Pedersen with his eyes.

"A couple of cows....that's all she had. And when did you make the discovery that there isn't any use for cows on a farm? And can you name me other places in Alberta where you can buy good milch cows *for eight dollars*. You can keep your coffee, and I hope you choke on it. You bandit! And you, Frederik! Be on your guard. You at any rate are not too old yet to be prevented from being jostled around."

Frederik drove his plug around in his mouth faster and faster. "You know you can just come along outside, you stuck-up Ross Dane who has to stick his nose in everything!"

"Well, heh, well, you know really now," Pedersen said, quietly laughing, "we certainly don't want any commotion. Of course Ross is completely mistaken...."

"Good. Will you sell the cows back to the woman for sixteen dollars?"

"Well, see a deal is a deal...."

"Theft," said Ross.

Frederik closed in on him.

"Out with you."

They both lifted their arms. At that very instant they stood firmly clasped, looking each other hatefully in the eyes.

107

"Bastard", snarled Frederik.

"Thief", said Rasmus.

They didn't move their legs, but their arms were tightened. Pedersen got up anxiously. He remembered what had once befallen Fyodor Murazezsky. He was never completely himself after having been squeezed by Ross Dane.

Theodor also stood up, but he remained standing calmly and looked on.

"Stop!" shouted Pedersen.

But they didn't let go. Both grew dark red in the face until Frederik suddenly became pale and opened his mouth with a gasp.

Ross let him down in a chair. Frederik breathed vehemently. His forehead was wet. *That* was the test of strength he had wanted for so long...

Theodor stepped over to Ross. He smiled and said with his hoarse, friendly voice,

"Do you have any cows to sell, Ross?"

"Perhaps I do."

"Can I buy two? You can decide the price."

Ross looked from Theodor to Frederik and Pedersen.

"That money you have on you is mine," said Pedersen, frightened.

"It *was* yours, father, but now they're an advance on the wages for that time I've worked here."

" *Advance... wages?*"

"Yes," answered Theodor in a friendly voice, "that's what I said. I have three hundred dollars on me. Is that too much?"

"Some day no doubt you'll get a share in the farm," said Pedersen, agitated, "so what...."

"You can keep your farm. I'll set myself up one. Can I ride with you, Ross? You can take my clothes in the wagon too, can't you? I hear you need a man."

Frederik and his father stood there deathly pale.

"You'll be remembered for this, you scoundrel," screamed Frederik. "You weakling, just a burden lying around here and...."

"And kept a man outside for four years," continued Theodor. "Well, this has got to end now. I've seen enough of farming *here*".

Pedersen stood by the window gazing after the wagon.

"There, he took Theodor," he said and stroked his beard. "Heh, well. That Theodor was never to my taste. But he was my son - and a good worker to have. We can poorly do without that money he ran off with."

"If he sells his inheritance for three hundred dollars, it's a good deal," said Frederik candidly. "But this day will be the dearest one Ross has lived through."

2.

Theodor worked during the fall over at Ross's. He bought land in remote North Coulee, a side valley of Beaver Coulee far away from people - and for the time being there wasn't much chance that anyone would come either, since everything, with the exception of what Theodor had bought, lay off in bog and scrub. He had an outhouse dragged out there which he had bought from Ross, and began on his own.

- - - -

Ross still had his first houses standing, but they were now inhabited by the animals of the farm. A new dwelling had been raised up on the edge of the prairie, and near it stood a large barn reminiscent of the nave of a church. Beaver Coulee had become a busy place, people came and went, conflicts were many. People were at odds with the grain buyers, and politics continually entered more strongly into everyday life.

Ross thought Eva was the same as when he had fetched her in Youngstown, and she too didn't seem to assume a view of her husband that was much different from before. But the honeymoon and all its flurry was only a memory of the past. Practical things had absorbed them both. She managed a large household and had three boys who went to school and who could only be distinguished from each other by their parents. Which of them was youngest or which eldest was not known. Fred, Chris and Pete were indeed a trinity. They as good as never used the singular about themselves; they had been born plural. From the beginning they caused their teacher the kind of distress which is a prerequisite for boys who are going to amount to something. When he called upon Chris, and Pete was better informed, he arose, prompted by Fred. And if one of them was caught playing pranks, all three maintained that it had to be one of the others. They virtually had command of the farm and were daring horsemen. Charles had instructed them in shooting, and had the praise of his pupils.

The boys had become a connecting link out to the other residents in Beaver Coulee. Often there wasn't time for visits over the great distances, or people didn't have an urge to see one another. But the boys continually brought tidings home so that Eva and Ross were never unfamiliar with public opinion in Beaver Coulee.

Many different kinds of people had arrived. The colony never became homogeneous. People of all nations constantly arrived, but Scandinavians were in the majority because a Galician colony not far to the south was more attractive to these people, and the Germans had a colony to the east. Ross lost his aversion to Swedes. They seemed in spite of his old experiences to be all right. But they blew trumpets and were Salvation men. That was a thorn in his side. Salvation people and freethinkers had never had his love. When Ross one evening heard the trumpets moan far away, he involuntarily reached for his rifle as in the old days when the coyotes were a plague in the land. Now coyotes were few, even though one almost always saw a couple in the winter when sledding grain to the station. They weren't loud or impertinent either any more, even if it could happen that they got troublesome. Rasmus remembered that he had promised to shoot some which were pillaging on Huseby's farm...

He got up one night, dressed himself as for an arctic expedition and turned his sheepskin coat inside out, as he regarded it as a fact that one sees no ghosts when one has got into his clothes the wrong way. The prairie lay in its white stillness, shiveringly cold. The waning moon sailed high. It looked as if it had lost its missing part by a straight, well-carried stroke of an axe. He caught himself letting his glance go searching over the sky for the amputated piece.

The tall, barrel-vaulted stalls became clear in the lines between the snow and the man. By the southern end of the barn stood a dozen horses which began carrying on a grumbling speech when he stepped out onto the farmyard. One thinks himself able to see a long way by the light of the moon, but Ross hadn't gone very far from the farm before the buildings simultaneously were dimmed and became transparent, while in a ravine between the prairie hills, down to which no moonray reached, things stood so that they could be taken by the glance without resistance.

The light of the snow wrestled under the sky with the moon's light and dispersed the lines of sight. A bridge of darkness shot itself through the air, and on it went the northern lights wavering from one horizon to another. It was as if in the moonlight nature too had put its fur on backward so that the darkness unveiled and the light concealed.

It soon struck him that he was alone. It wasn't the usual feeling of loneliness which is independent of the presence of other people, but another, a certainty that here he moved, he alone. All others were sleeping. What he was doing would remain unknown by everybody as long as he wished. Here no mask need be worn. It was with a feeling of satisfaction, he found, that he was still the same as otherwise, he wasn't doing anything extraordinary, he was walking quite naturally on his legs! He was out to shoot coyotes, the tracks of which stood in the snow each morning in a bog toward the northwest, and which several times had been seen there at daybreak - and which stole Huseby's poultry. It was so natural and simple out here. He didn't suddenly begin making flying movements or snarling and hissing like a badger. The world became whiter. The prairie spread out like a pale, sleeping face, the northern lights grew tremblingly higher. It was in the last third of the night when the cold digs in its teeth. The snow puffed up like dust where he stepped. The northern lights sloped downward and built a golden way right across the sky. On it the Big Dipper remained still.

Out in the frozen bog he crept into a bush, rolled his blanket around his legs and sat quietly. Somewhat later the northern lights left the sky, the moon went away, it grew dark. But the white snow kept the darkness from the earth. The night hung down toward the whiteness like the stalagtite formations in a cave. And it was as if the white prairie hills began to breathe, to rise and fall like the breast of a sleeping person. He closed his eyes and felt how still the night was.

Like down an owl floated past him several times. It had surely seen him but went about its business without taking notice of him. And when it had been forgotten that a human being had come to the place, he beheld how full of hares the prairie was. One didn't see them so much before the snow levelled the land out, but constantly now he had two, three or four within sight. Then they were gone. He didn't see that they ran, hid themselves, or how it happened. They sort of explained themselves away. They were gone, and only the owl silently kept him company.

A quarter hour after the hares' disappearance the coyotes ran into the hollow in front of him, one large one and two smaller ones. His shots couldn't fail to hit them, and therefore he waited, wanting to use the opportunity to see the nocturnal howlers at close range. Straight away they stood still, the smaller ones on either side of the large one. Their heads they held in the air so that the white underside from the throat to the nose showed itself as three light triangles. They stood without moving a hair. It was the small one on the left that broke the immobility. It moved quickly three or four yards diagonally forward, turned and looked back, turned itself around, stood still again and slowly moved its head in almost a complete revolution. The others walked forward and did the same. Then they restlessly began searching the hollow.

Next he saw a remarkable sight: when the coyotes were in the middle of the little valley something began moving over from where they had come. It glided slowly up along the slope, on the top of which it appeared for a moment more sharply and then disappeared. It was a hare! The coyote had never stood high in his esteem, but after seeing this it fell abysmally. He shot just as much out of indignation and contempt as in an effort to get the animals. The old one fell under the first shot, one of the young ones under the second. The third coyote took off. When he got to his feet he saw something streak over a hillcrest further off. He shot, but hit nothing.

He hung the coyotes on his back and walked toward the Huseby farm. In the dawn it was clouding over for snow. A flight of crows flew past him morning low; the winter made them brazen. Their audacious voices still rang after him when he came into the farmyard. There he put the coyotes on the steps while he made himself free of his heavy outdoor things. He had become extremely hungry and was contemplating what might be offered for breakfast. A dog came running and looked at its dead cousins. It bared its teeth in a cruel grin, but kept itself a couple of paces away. Then it came over to Ross, wagged its tail and cast a sidelong glance at the fallen ones. He hadn't seen that dog with such an expressive look before and didn't really like it afterward.

The farm wife stepped out onto the veranda to get a bucket and greeted him good morning.

"Here you can see," he said. "It was a cold night, but it paid off. Coyote meat can very well be eaten if you're hungry enough. It tastes like printer's ink."

She threw a wincing glance at the pile.

"Take it away," she said vehemently.

He took the animals away, carried them over into the barn and didn't think any further about her testiness. There were of course people who couldn't bear seeing a dead fly. But a little later he saw her standing staring out into the prairie. There was a haunted look in her eyes. Something dawned on Ross. In the farmyard he met the husband, who remained standing as if unsure. He wanted to say something, but was searching for words.

"Here...here we are in the habit of... when we have caught an animal, we go into the barn with it from the south, you know. And let it stay there."

"Your wife can't stand...?" asked Ross carefully.

"She can slaughter a bull."

Ross stood silent.

"But you see...when we came here...she of course longed to go home to Bergen. There was water there, you see. Here there is only prairie. And all the strange things we can get in from out there..."

He stopped resignedly, couldn't get his ideas sheathed by words.

"Is she afraid of the prairie?"

His eyes perked up.

"Yes, exactly, that's just it. *She's afraid of the prairie.* We men don't understand that sort of thing of course, do we? But she is, however much we talk...afraid of the prairie..."

He went, and Ross was left standing, strangely affected. Slowly he sauntered over into the barn and looked a while at the dead coyotes which lay senselessly gaping with fixed hate and hunger in their glazed eyes. He wanted to shake something oppressive off himself but couldn't and hardly knew what it was. He had again met something which momentarily could become visible in women who were getting on a little in years before they came to this country. He didn't understand it. But there were many things which Ross didn't understand and yet which in the course of the years he had learned to reckon with anyway.

3.

With four horses in front of the heavy grain-laden sled Ross was on his way to town. The sled runners shrieked against the frozen snow. It was quiet weather, cuttingly cold. Much of the time he waded in the tall drifts to keep warm and took a rest only when his lungs no longer were up to such violent exertion in the thin air. He was thinking about how prices would stand this year. Last fall they had been low, but later this was discovered to be a local phenomenon - the grain buyers had the remotely lying colonies by the short hairs. They had had a good harvest, but it had become a poor year anyway.

How would it go this year? It had been a rather poor harvest, but surely it was like that everywhere in Canada, and it should mean slightly higher prices....

Sleds came toward him over between the hills. It was Fyodor and Huseby, who were on their way home. They were the first ones who had been in with grain.

Ross drove his sled off to the side of the road to ask the news. Then he saw that the sleds were heavy and full. His face darkened.

Fyodor came first. He struck the rimy horses so that they came past Ross at a trot. The two men looked each other in the eyes as they passed by, they measured and weighed old hatred. But Huseby pulled up.

"You seem to be hauling grain to the farm when others are hauling it away, Eugen Huseby!"

Huseby took off his mittens and let the kernels filter through his fingers.

"I am, and others will do it too," he said, indignant. "They're offering thirty-five cents a bushel."

Ross pulled his beard into his mouth and chewed on it. He sat silent for a long time. That price would mean that one could live precisely until next fall, but no longer, if one were free of debts. There'd be hardship in Beaver Coulee. One year's slavery for the grain merchants. His first impulse was to sled on in and beat the brains out of a couple of them. But then he began to think. He turned his horses and went home behind Huseby.

115

For several days they bided their time. Ross was working on a plan whereby those who were better off would form a trust, so that the poorer ones could not be forced to sell right away. But Pedersen was unwilling. Why, that would just be loaning money to people who perhaps would never pay it back. Could you trust just anyone like that?

Ivan then proposed isolating Pedersen. He himself would contribute a thousand dollars. Ross put another thousand on the table. But no one else joined them. Fyodor said no, Huseby said no - no down the whole line. Then Ivan and Ross joined forces. They proclaimed that they had established "Beaver Coulee Grain Purchasing", which would buy wheat at seventy-five cents a bushel, but not from those who had refused to go in on the first projected pact. The sellers committed themselves before spring to hauling the sold wheat to the station.

A week later a visitor came to the valley, an emissary from the grain merchants. He paid Ross a visit, wanted to correct various misunderstandings which had crept in. Those thirty-five cents were not at all to be considered as a final price, but as a payment on account. Because of the fluctuating quotations they didn't dare fix a price now. They were sorry about the affair especially because it seemed as though King Dane were offended. Why was he? Always before they had traded in friendliness, but this year Ross hadn't been in town at all. Why was the king offended?

Ross was very friendly. He understood so well this matter of fluctuating quotations. That was why they wanted to wait to sell until the price became firm. But you see - there are of course people who can't wait - and that's something you haven't thought about at all in town.

The man sat a bit and reflected. He was not really in the mood to accept the theory of his bosses' lack of consideration, for neither he nor Ross was a child. He made some vague comments and stated that of course they only did business with producers, not with competing buyers. We are people with principles, King Dane, and these we have to stick to.

But Ross looked unsympathetically at him. He couldn't see what that had to do with the matter. "Beaver Coulee Grain Purchasing" didn't buy from buyers either...

The man bit his lip. His thoughts took another turn. How much I wonder could those people get together, did they have the capital, could themselves send the grain to the east? In such a case what would one's position be? - first with regard to his profit, then with regard to his name?

He was over talking with Ivan. The man was of course a Galician and most likely an oaf - but Ivan just mumbled and was deferential, as was fitting for a Galician - well, ha, bah - he needed a lot of wheat - fattening of oxen - with wheat, certainly not a bad idea, and a bread factory, hm, hm, but capital is scarce. If it were possible perhaps to float a little loan in town?

The grain merchant cleared out. He felt quite sheepish and never afterward embarked on negotiation with the Galician Ivan.

- - -

The prices rose a bit in town, but no one came with wheat. Fyodor walked around wild and furious on his farm, Huseby shut himself up, Pedersen stroked his beard, his eyes wandered, this indeed did not seem promising, and look at those crazy people Ross and Ivan, did they want with brute force to upset everything? Heh, heh, it was indeed a time of prosperity for those who had been on the point of going bankrupt, *they* were earning money this year...but the end was very likely drawing near for King Dane and Ivan. Pedersen knew better than anyone what those people were worth in ready money. Now your back will soon break, Ross Dane!

- - -

Several weeks passed. Pedersen was standing one day looking over at the king's houses outlined audaciously high and bright in the lines under the winter sky. Yes, always pushing up into the clouds over at that Ross's! What could that property actually be got for at a forced sale? What indeed was that little Frederik plotting? Pedersen didn't let on his being curious, but he knew Frederik was active. Heh, heh, that Frederik, he had brains, that was certain. Didn't he go to town yesterday and put good money in the bank? And didn't the amount correspond to a nice price on what had disappeared from the granaries? Heh, heh, one wasn't cheated with such a son. He was inside sleeping now in the middle of the day, but Pedersen didn't blame him. For Frederik of course went outside looking at stars at night. Heh, heh, Frederik loved nature. Wasn't it brightening up for folks in Beaver Coulee? Wasn't that Fyodor Murazezsky going around looking happy? Pedersen stroked his beard. Yes indeed, heaven gave a crop, and it gave money in the cash box - in sunny Alberta!

Ross Dane came riding over to Ivan's. They spoke a little about trivial things, then Ivan looked straight at Ross: "I'm ruined now, Ross Dane, if we don't get good news from the East."

Ross looked out the window for a while.

"Yes, we two are in the same boat," he said.

There was a long pause. Then Ross said,

"But Ivan, I had some business over here. We thought it was a bad year,

117

didn't we?"

"I've thought about that," said Ivan.

"Me too. And I saw there had to be something wrong. There were people who *couldn't* have had so large a harvest. We've been duped, Ivan. We've bought wheat for an excess price at Frederik's and Fyodor's."

Ivan shoved the chair back and got up. His face was like a baited tiger's.

"Which...which one of them we have helped has...we've ruined ourselves for...oh, those bastards," he moaned, "which one of them could go along with that trick after we saved...saved them all?"

"That's what I thought last night," Ross almost whispered, "when I began putting two and two together. Ivan, they have all been in on it, *all of them!* They have all hauled Fyodor's and Frederik's wheat to our granaries. Outside are only Huseby and the others we didn't want to buy from. They certainly don't know anything - otherwise we too would probably have....well."

He sighed. Then he saw the tears run down old Ivan's cheeks. At that sight he felt his own eyes become wet. But still his features were calm when he stepped over and put a hand on the Galician's shoulder.

"Humans are the spawn of the devil," he said quietly. "But now I'll tell you something, my friend, now that you've been through what I endured last night while I thought that my wife and children would be turned out... Now we've learned that he who gives until he begs, will be struck down right off his legs."

His voice rose triumphantly:

"But...we have learned that, Ivan, without getting the bitter end along with it. Ivan, damn it! Stand up and sing. The news from the whole country is getting darker and darker. The harvest has been a complete failure out in Manitoba, in Saskatchewan it's bad, in the States even worse. It's nothing to shout with joy about...no...but our corner in wheat has turned out lucky. There was a man with me this morning. I sold him the whole lot for two dollars a bushel! Damn it, I got the last of Fyodor's along with it... All those bastards, they wanted to have us go begging from Beaver Coulee. Now we can...well, what can we do? We can in any case buy a couple of flag poles. For a long time I have wanted a flag pole. Shall we buy two flag poles on 'Beaver Coulee Grain Purchasing's' bill, Ivan?"

Ivan stood reeling and held on to the edge of the table. Then he walked slowly into another room and softly closed the door behind him. In there Ross knew hung a picture of the mother of God. And now he heard Ivan give thanks for his deliverance. The Galician's voice resounded excitedly, his tone almost cracking from sentence to sentence. First he said a few words in English, then mixed his own language into it until it became pure Polish. But the beginning had given Ross a key to understanding, and he recognized many of the Polish words in what followed. Those he didn't understand literally he guessed at while Ivan's voice sank to a mumble.

"Holy mother of God, give me strength so I can forgive my enemies. I thank you because you didn't let us be robbed of everything in this heartless land... Each cent of all that money which has undeservedly come to my unworthy self today shall be given toward a church in my countrymen's colony. And thank you because Ross Dane was spared. You look into our hearts and know that he is good. Give us good health, give us good years. You know I only wish those riches my hands make..."

Then Ross sat down and cried from happiness and emotion. And he cried from shame. Was that man in there not a Galician? Ross hated himself, his race. Here the Scandinavian people went around being self-important and imagining the planet was theirs, swaggering because their eyes were blue and their hair blond, heh, as if those were especially lovely colours! Wouldn't green hair have been more chic, purple eyes? - and imagine if one had a prehensile tail. That would be handsome. Then people could pull each other's tail. Fyodor, the Galician Fyodor, was supposed to be a damned scum, but just look at Frederik Pedersen... Set that Dane up against the Galician Ivan!

- - -

The first one who turned up when the grain reversal was rumoured was Eugen Huseby. He sat for a while at Ross's, then started to leave without having said much. But as the Norwegian took the handle of the door, he said,

"You were lucky, Ross Dane. All the same it wasn't right of you to stake your existence on one card. Now you've won in a big way."

"And those who were badly off are saved, Huseby!"

"You'll see what thanks you'll get now."

"I *have* got it."

"Much good may it do you. I am happy now that no one owes me revenge in acknowledgement. I have sold well today. Those of us who didn't want to go along that time - Fyodor, Pedersen and the others - we can be satisfied now."

Ross laughed. "Yes, ask them!" he said. "I'm not sure they're so downright overjoyed. Incidentally, a whole deputation is coming from down there. They're coming up to King Dane to get a share of the booty. You can ask them why Frederik and Fyodor aren't along."

"Frederik and Fyodor...?"

"Well, I'm going to the school to pick up the triplets so goodby to you! See to it that you ask them nicely: Why aren't Frederik and Fyodor along?"

Ross stood at the window and followed Huseby with his eyes as he stopped and talked with those coming. They shifted so uneasily on their feet and looked up at the farm. When Huseby left them they didn't speak to each other but drifted off each in his own direction.

Then Ross Dane laughed. Tomorrow he'd send word that grain was going to be hauled. A shame that Frederik and Fyodor hadn't come along!

- - -

Theodor arrived for a visit several days later, but didn't find Ross at home. Eva received him in a friendly way. Theodor began talking about Ivan's and Ross's corner in wheat. Why not be generous? Give them the surplus - heavens, they haven't any idea at all what they've done!

"Fyodor and your brother should probably have a taste too?"

Theodor became red.

"I know that Frederik is my brother," he said curtly. "He's on the point of bringing an action."

"Against whom?"

"Against Ross. He maintains that Ross knew very well when he sold his wheat where the last of it had come from. And it was Ross's duty then according to the contract not to accept it. Now Frederik wants compensation."

"Wouldn't it have been much easier for Frederik to have kept his wheat at home? But let's see now - Ross won't at any rate distribute any money until he's seen how great a compensation Frederik wants. And Fyodor..."

Theodor was silent. He followed Eva with his eyes. It was always strange to see her. For he knew of course that she was that woman he had once loved. Though *was* it Eva? It was and it wasn't. Her name could make him tremble. But now the name didn't apply at all to the present Eva - it applied to the strong girl who long ago had come with Ross Dane to Beaver Coulee. Theodor didn't love Eva Dane. But he could never forget that girl he had once loved, a woman who could never be gained, for she *wasn't* any longer, she had become a poem and a dream, grown out of the visions here in the valleys, created by night's concupiscence and all the years' changing days which had whispered a single woman's name. To her he could never stretch out his arms. He had desired the world and got a vision.

But lately the vision had been on the way back to earth. A brother of Eugen Huseby, Sigurd, had come up from the States to farm in the district, and he had brought his sister over from Norway as his housekeeper. Her name was Kaja. Theodor was overwhelmed when he saw her. She was indeed another Eva. Others would scarcely happen on that thought, and Theodor himself couldn't account for it. To be sure she was strong, big and blonde like Eva, but

120

otherwise didn't resemble her. It was probably something or other in a movement, a glance or whatever that reminded him of Eva from one occasion or another while he had lain eaten up with tuberculosis in the latticed cage on his father's farm. Kaja gave him a lot to think about. She complicated his thoughts as quickly as she created them in him. He wasn't capable of keeping her apart from the memory of Eva, of Eva then and Eva now. He longed for Kaja, whenever he sat alone out in North Coulee, for she was Eva who young and recreated was present on Huseby's farm. But if he came and saw her, he felt in himself a disappointment and powerlessness. He became weak. She wasn't Eva. Anyway he came often. For he noticed that she wasn't tired of it, she was friendly and held him back if he wanted to leave again too soon.

Sigurd Huseby, though, certainly didn't like Theodor's visits. His eyes moved restlessly under his bushy brow whenever Theodor was in the room, and he was fond of talking negatively about Danes. He often obliged with some historical scraps which were supposed to prove that Danes were degenerate descendants of Norwegians, and he also adopted a patronizing manner as if he were Theodor's forefather forty times removed. Sigurd in no way resembled his brother Eugen, in whose character the lines were as straight as if drawn with a ruler. One suspected pitfalls on Sigurd Huseby's farm.

But Eva - no, he meant Kaja - was so still and quiet. It was restful to be with her. And Theodor got up abruptly, asked Eva to give Ross his greetings, took his horse and rode over to Sigurd Huseby's.

Sigurd and his sister lived in a large log cabin which was used for services whenever an itinerant preacher came to the colony. Theodor didn't like that type of house. Why hadn't Sigurd made rooms? Sigurd was master here; nothing could happen which he wasn't aware of. It was another matter with Theodor and many other beginners - they also had just one room, but they were alone and poor. Sigurd was neither, and he hadn't been when he was building, either.

At Sigurd's the business of Ross Dane's and Ivan's grain sale was discussed.

"There you can see the work of foxes!" said Sigurd. "Thank God I kept out of it. All those poor people plundered!"

"If 'Beaver Coulee Grain Purchasing' hadn't existed, they'd only have got half the price," answered Theodor. "And shrewd people like Frederik and Fyodor - they..."

"Bah," interrupted Sigurd, "the shrewder ones swindle the less shrewd ones. Frederik and Fyodor cheated themselves into being cheated, that's all."

"I don't feel sorry for anybody," declared Theodor. "Most of the colony let themselves be helped and laughed at Ross and Ivan behind their backs. Then they let themselves be paid by Frederik and Fyodor to swindle the benefactors.

And if it had been left up to the colony and the town's grain merchants, two farms would now be have been up for forced sale - after having saved all the others. That a miracle occurred in the end, honourable people are glad of. No one has suffered by it."

"That's right," said Kaja.

Sigurd looked up quickly, but said nothing more about it. Theodor felt himself warmed by her words. Sigurd went out soon afterward, but his eyes stayed on Theodor and his sister until the door had closed.

Kaja worked at the stove. She was baking bread. Theodor remembered how once as a little boy he had been beside himself with fright at seeing his mother's hands go into the dough. He had got the idea that they were lost forever. He had shook the whole day after that experience. Now he couldn't at all recall that feeling though the image was the same as then. Kaja made her fingers free of the dough, sprinkled flour on it, rolled the lump and kneaded again. The sight had such a calming effect, it hypnotized, it was as if all his life, for a whole eternity, he had known nothing but a woman kneading dough.

"You're not saying anything," said Kaja.

"No!" he said, groping. "I feel so comfortable just being allowed to sit and look at you."

It was not at all meant in the way she would have to understand it. But the only reasonable explanation of the words didn't dawn on him.

She didn't say anything, and he remained sitting, rocking with the chair. A bit later he began to speak.

"You know very likely that I haven't always been as I am now. I have stamina now and can keep pace with any fellow. I probably look thin, but there are sinews through my whole body. When I was lying for two years in an open house over at father's it was different. Then Eva Dane came over sometimes and made my bed. She took me like a child and laid me over in a corner. You know, I was then just as tall as she. You're not going to go around making fun of that sort of thing, are you? But I fell in love with Eva Dane."

A moment later he continued,

"You resemble her - as she was then."

That was meant as a compliment. He himself found it a considerable one. Therefore he didn't comprehend why she looked disappointed. Well, so she resembled the one he couldn't have.

But Theodor didn't touch further on this difficult problem about those two who each minute became one and became two again. He looked around in the room and grew disconsolate.

He got up, cut a chip off a log and stuck it in his mouth. Theodor neither chewed tobacco nor smoked, but he ate pine chips. It was good for the lungs,

Charles had said, and the lungs are the most important thing in the whole body, enclosed wings of sorts to fan air around the heart with.

Theodor began to think about that and said suddenly:

"Then the angels must have their hearts hanging on their backs."

Kaja looked at him in surprise. But he spoke on. "It's certainly not good for me to be alone out in North Coulee. When I was sick, I began to hear and see many strange things. This starts to crop up again now that I'm alone. No, it's not good for a person to be alone."

Kaja slowly drew her fingers out of the dough, wiped them off and went over to him. Her voice was unsteady.

"You always say so much that sets me thinking, but then you can suddenly say that it's nice weather - and go away. Perhaps I don't really understand you. Are you fond of me, Theodor?"

He became terrified. Now there it was! He hadn't thought anything through, neither half nor whole, just thought aloud, because it was so pleasant near her.

"Yes, Kaja, I am. But it...I..."

"Why don't you say it then?"

"Why I did. I said yes."

She looked at him and came without knowing why to think of a story she had once read about a young man who had been found in Germany somewhere. He was so ignorant of everything like a little child. She had felt so sorry for him. His name had been Kasper, a name that made her feel maternal, too. Theodor was very wise. Everyone knew that. He could enjoy books which for others were only a mass of words and numbers put together without meaning. He was a lawyer for the farmers and could survey land. But in love he was a Kasper.

She straightened his coat collar a little. "You should take me away from here, Theodor."

"Yes, but I have neither money nor house of course. Just a shed - why you know that."

He gently put his hand on her arm and stroked it. "You aren't to believe in that story about a hearth and home, Kaja. I want a harvest before I come for you."

"Are you able to wait?" she asked impetuously.

"Yes, I can do that."

Angrily she turned away from him, didn't see the glow that burst out in his eyes: "Eva, Eva!" But when she looked at him again he was once more - Kasper.

She thought she could say whatever it might be.

"I *must* get away from here, Theodor. I've been here too long..."

Crying, she fell down in front of the chair and grasped his knee. Too long?

123

he thought, and felt a gray shadow in his heart. Then he didn't want to take her away from here.

He remained sitting and slowly let his hands go over her hair. She became calmer, lifted her head and looked at him. He didn't say anything. There was nothing to read in his face. Then she got up and went over to her work. When he rode from the farm she said goodby kindly and asked him to come back soon.

4.

The day Ross Dane was to appear in town to answer Frederik's summons he drove from home in good time with his boys. Eva wondered why they were going along. Was a lawsuit anything for them? But he laughed and chucked her under the chin - you're getting fat, mummy, and don't understand fun any more! The triplets are going to see how a scoundrel is treated!

When Ross was well along the main road he stopped the sled and said, "Chris, Fred and Pete, you know what Frederik and Fyodor did to us, and you know why we're out driving today. You see what I have here? It's a good birch rod. One like this was worn out on my backend when I was your age every time I played some of those tricks that you now go around imitating every day. The reason you don't get the rod is because it hasn't improved me. You've heard your mother say that often enough, so I'm sure it's true. But you see, if you don't get the rod now, and later on it appears that you actually ought to have had it, then you'll get it as grownups. See Frederik, he never got the rod as a child. Therefore he's getting it today. Out with you and have a snowball fight so you can keep warm. When Frederik comes you'll get a dose of fear and warning."

When Frederik's sled appeared, Ross reined the horses in so that the road was blocked. Frederik stopped. His jaws began working.

"I just wanted to talk a bit with you before the lawsuit," said Ross.

"I dare say you'll get the opportunity to talk in town, you swindler," shouted Frederik. "Out of the way! Otherwise you'll get your horses scattered."

He swung his whip, but before the blow fell, Ross grabbed the horses' headgear. They reared wildly, sweeping Ross along into the air, but he came down on his feet again and his own horses got such a blow and a fright that they went into the ditch. The sled blocked the road now. It would be Frederik's funeral if he kept at it.

Frederik's jaws revolved like millstones. His eyes flashed.

"Come down then and talk, little Frederik."

But he stayed where he was, standing with the whip and watching for Ross to come close enough. This will take too long, thought Ross, and picked up his own whip and began fencing with Frederik. Chris, Fred and Pete looked on from the top of a snowdrift. They shouted hurrah whenever Frederik got a flick of the whip, they howled in rage whenever their father got one. Right in by the wagon Ross got hold of the end of Frederik's whip, then let go of his own and pulled. But Frederik had the better grip, and pulled desperately until Ross let go. Frederik's legs went into the air, and before he had got up again, Ross's fingers lay around his throat.

"Well, so you're going to sue folks, little Frederik? You damned cheat stealing from widows and trying to save your harvest by robbing your neighbour who's on the edge of bankruptcy...Fred, Chris and Pete!"

The boys came rushing.

"Take the rope in the sled and tie his legs together. There's a noose in it so it'll be easy."

Frederik tried to kick, but Ross squeezed hard. Frederik had to let the boys tie him. Then Ross turned him around and pushed him half out of the sled so that he hung in a suitable position, unbuckled his belt and made additional preparations for the execution. Frederik protested furiously. But Ross picked up the birch rod and wore it out while Frederik's screams echoed among the hills.

- - -

Frederik sledded home at a gallop. He couldn't show himself anywhere that day. Whipping can be bad enough in itself, but if it's going to happen under open sky when the Celsius thermometre shows 35 degrees below zero it's a martyrdom. He failed to appear in court. The next day the sheriff came and apprehended Ross Dane.

The punishment was set at $500 in fines and $200 to Frederik for damages.

"This isn't quite as I had imagined," said Ross.

"No, now you may fork out," gloated Frederik.

"That man misunderstands the situation entirely," said Ross. "I had set aside $1000 before I flogged him. I only wish I had known before I let him go that I still had $300 worth of spanking left"

Frederik turned green. From that day on all contact was broken between the colony's founders. Chris, Fred and Pete kept far away from Pedersen's farm. Frederik took back his summons against Ross when the magistrate asked him if he hadn't made enough of a fool of himself this round.

Pedersen aged somewhat during those days. Heh, that Ross! First he took a son from him, then took the profit from a high-paid harvest. Then he made the other son impossible to live with so that he was now more occupied consulting with Fyodor than with looking after the farm. Hadn't Pedersen once said clearly enough to Fyodor that in Beaver Coulee it wasn't advisable to quarrel with Ross Dane? But youth never wanted to listen to experienced people's talk. Ross, that idiot - to assault people even when he knew it would be so expensive, that was crazy. No, now there had been enough hullabaloo, it would be good if Frederik amicably went over and spoke with the king. Of course one also had to consider that Ross and Ivan were strong now. Heaven had let it rain dollars over them, alas yes. Pedersen looked over toward Ross Dane's farm: the flag was flying. It must be Eva's birthday. A flag like that cost seven dollars, they said in town. Heh, there came Frederik and Fyodor. They too cast a sidelong glance at the flag.

Bitterly Pedersen turned away. His son had behaved foolishly. What was he gaping at a flag for? Better to go up and speak with Ross and say this, that - and - the other. Heh, stand glowering at a flag - he was still standing there, the fool. He could go inside and look at his rear end in the mirror, then he'd see flags, both the Danish flag and the Stars and Stripes. That was all one got out of fighting with Ross Dane. Who else in the world besides Ross Dane could produce triplets and earn money on charity and still be free of ulterior motives? No, Frederik spoiled the whole design here in sunny Alberta.

- - -

The following spring the first cars came to Beaver Coulee. About a dozen appeared at one time; presumably everyone had thought of surprising everyone else. It was strange that the first one who came sweeping through the country in a motor vehicle was the Metis Charles Villeneuve. That was the proper vehicle for him when he was going to pick up a moose in the north. Charles was a hunter. He never became anything else, however much he pretended to be a farmer.

Immediately motoring led to many foolish things. The car was still too new not to be first and foremost a form of boasting. An enormously tall Copenhagener, who like Charles pretended to be a farmer, but didn't know anything about hunting, threw himself into cars. He had never earned a cent, but received money from Denmark, presumably a rich man's son whom somebody in Copenhagen would rather see stay in sunny Alberta. Now he became of use in the world by introducing the varying types of cars to the inhabitants of Beaver Coulee. That was enough to make him ridiculous. But it grew worse when he got his hitherto flashiest model home but couldn't drive it because his legs were

127

so long that his knees stuck up between the spokes of the steering wheel. After that the farmers in the area always used a piece of twine to measure whether their legs could fit under the steering wheel before they bought a car.

The newness quickly wore off the cars, though. They entered into daily life in the course of a month. And the prairie remained the same, naked, rolling, lonely.

Feuding continued that summer, but there was already some class division, though it didn't reveal itself in social conversation - and it was the big ones who fought, the little ones who looked on. A man who one night struck matches by a stack of straw lying up against Ross Dane's barn got his jawbone ripped open by a rifle bullet. No one knew him, and he admitted nothing. Ross let him go with what he had got.

A growing stream of emigrants came to the place. Continually the Danes were preponderate, since by now the Norwegians had formed their own colony also in the district. But the young farmhands went off where there was work to be got; they were the restless and mixed element in all colonies. The old colonists were displeased with youth; the farmhands talked about loneliness and boredom, "It is certainly sad here too in contrast to the old days. Then you should have seen us out here, said Ross - we hibernated in the winter like the badger. Freethinker Jensen used to lie in his bed for several months staring at the door until his thoughts at last fastened on to it in a big, lavish painting. In those days coyotes with human heads and without tails went here, but they died out when the devil took the freethinker. One of them I shot where Fyodor is farming now. Its soul has gone into him, that's clear. How can anyone be a freethinker when he sees something so obvious? You're deaf and dumb if you can't see it - Fyodor is descended from a coyote and Frederik from a badger. Only good Christians aren't descended from anything. Now people come running and are freethinkers every other one, or they blow trumpets. You scamps have time for all sorts of things nowadays. Here we take the Lord as he always has been - that's both simplest and cheapest. No, whenever I think about freethinker Jensen, then I really know, for it would be bloody injustice if there isn't a Hell to put him in. If you could lay off your free thinking and curl your thumbs, then it would never occur to you that it's sad on the prairie. You are dead lazy. That's all."

Ross conducted many such speeches as he sat at the end of the table and looked at the twelve to fourteen farmhands who in busy times ate at his table. Half of them hated him; for the other half he was an idol. But no one remained untouched by King Dane. He was too much alive.

5.

Theodor still lived and worked in out-of-the-way North Coulee where people almost never came. Out there the land lay forgotten and reminded one of the times when a dozen Indians could pass through on a summer day each century, otherwise there had been quiet, eternal quiet. Confronted by this eternity a thought grew in Theodor that nothing was impossible. Everything could happen, and everything would happen. Events that wouldn't come couldn't be dreamed about. Human fantasy was the frame around what would happen. Everything humans had dreamed was true. Everything that hadn't happened until today would happen in coming days. People went around in miraculous, light-ravaged cities which had robbed them of the ability to see. The greater the miracles that happened, the lesser would be man's ability to see. In the end everything had happened, and man had become a vegetating plant.

In North Coulee Theodor lived through the seasons and lived with them. Whenever there was nothing else to do he drifted about with his rifle and reflected on Kaja, Eva and the Coulee. He didn't shoot much, but a grown man couldn't of course walk just for the sake of walking. And he took a rabbit home for himself now and then. He lived with the small things. Many days on end he went up onto the prairie to a rush bordered waterhole where there lay the skeleton of a horse. One could still espy the animal's shape in the bones which lay over the fat pile of topsoil which once had been a horse. The corpse head's stupid grin said blasphemically: Memento mori - you must remember that the world is a vast prairie full of will-o'-the-wisps which are lit and extinguished with pain. But the prairie remains eternally.

For a time it remained for him the whole world: The Prairie, a horse skeleton. In front of him lay his dirty, blood-stained working gloves. They had a living form and lay like two severed hands over the butt of his gun.

One day while he was away a preacher had come and painted on a stone. Here of course no one crowded around when somebody began to speak;

therefore the preacher worked with brush and paint pot. Theodor read: Oh, oh, oh yes, Jesus Christ is the cornerstone. This had been begun with letters so large that the last ones had to be made small and cramped in order to fit. Theodor became strangely embarrassed looking at this work of art, and after a couple of days he knocked over the stone. The painter must have seen this on the way back, for one fine morning there stood on the wall of Theodor's house in two-feet-high letters which also got too large and had to be reduced at the end: Good friend, how are you with eternity? You go assuredly to the dogs.

That Theodor regarded as not improbable. He felt divided, never happy. Both living and dead things told him something. Whenever he looked at the great wise owl sleeping on a dead tree's single branch not far from the cabin, then it was as if there came an emanation from it - we two, Theodor, we live with the coulee, we will never be happy. One day he had had enough of it and wanted to shoot the bird, but it suspected mischief and flew off. Shortly afterward he shot it down from a stack of straw. It wasn't dead when he came over to it. It got half up and turned its shaggy old man's face toward him, opened its broad mouth under the ferocious curve of its beak, and he read in its wild eyes: Theodor, you will never be happy.

In the winter, when the sun was just setting and its rays bathed the most distant prairie hills, then they didn't become white but bloody red, and the unthreshed grain out there on the curve of the hill stood like red, pointed beacons, the earth which had risen in tongues of fire. And then it shone over to him: Theodor, you will never be happy.

By the foot of hills lay petrified bones of the dinosaur. Theodor weighed them in his hand and thought about time. Now the coyote moved in Alberta's coulees. It would not die because it was too big, like the dinosaur, but die it would and be forgotten. Now rifle bullets sang on the prairie. There was sadness in that too, though he hated the coyote. It could stray onto the roof of his house when the drifts were high and howl there, the coyote, the hetaera of the prairie.

But there were also light elves. In a crack into a space in the roof stray pigeons lived. It made him happy to see them romp around his dwelling. When the mottled birds were out flying in a snowstorm, a part of their colour melted into the background, so that it came to look as if there were only a fragment of each single bird. It made him remember a Danish butcher's assistant who had sported a mottled calfskin vest. Even at quite a short range it looked as though the brown patches were holes.

And the snow bunting came in large flocks, flushing up and down in the air, but highest in the air each one flung its wings around, flushed in its individual direction so that the whole thing came to have the effect of a pile of paper scattered by a whirlwind. Then it could become three flocks that threw themselves down and again became one.

Whenever he walked in the bottom of the coulee and saw the slopes on both sides, he got the feeling that there were two lands which for millennia had been on a slow walk over toward each other and one day would meet. And with eyes up over the enormous curves of the hills he felt how there came to be meaning in a hackneyed phrase: A virgin land. The coulee bewitched him, it made him melancholy, but he loved it. At times it could nevertheless tire him out. There stood the coulee's rounded slope silhouetted against the night's quiet sky as the uppermost of many giants' heads. Owls screamed, and coyotes answered in distorted echo. He saw before him the clouds torn away under a Danish autumn sky over naked woods, heard water purl in ditches. During the nights there was light from many windowpanes. He saw Denmark with house beside house. His heart sighed. He wished himself away from the wild prairie and home in Denmark.

- - -

Time passed. While Theodor became in many ways more detached from reality than before, he got himself well started as a farmer. He was a persevering and hard-working man. He visited Kaja often, but more rarely went to see others in the colony. Only Ross Dane got a visit from him now and then. For a long time nothing happened between Kaja and Theodor. She shut herself off, and he was very careful. In her thoughts she always called him Kasper, little Kasper. But she was also afraid of him, and whenever he wasn't looking at her, she observed him with a puzzling glance. Who was he, what was he? She was insecure. After all it was not easy to understand someone else. Perhaps it meant a great deal that he had been in this country since he was a boy. Certainly that would give him a peculiar disposition.

The winter after she tried to have it out with Theodor, she noticed a great change in him. He became preoccupied and was no longer so careful about what he said. She thought that he had now found himself and no longer considered tying himself to her. But should she help him? Was it not she who had proposed to him and received humiliating evasions in reply?

Theodor carried on a bitter battle. He needed help, he needed Kaja. His brain kept reminding him of the brutal and smarting fact that it had lasted too long. Too long, too long, what had she actually said? He tried to interpret and change her words, but constantly they came back new and fresh, demanded a place again: I have been here too long. And Eva, Eva I see no way out with you, Eva...

But he was feeling a pressure that would disperse all considerations. For

Theodor was in distress.

People in the colony began to sense Theodor's anxiety after accompanying him whenever he walked to and from his cabin in the valley. They took care not to say anything to him about it and didn't speak about it mutually either. But whenever they talked together, and Theodor was mentioned, it was as if a strange person had walked through the living room.

One day Charles rode to North Coulee, and he saw how remarkably glad Theodor became. A happy glint appeared in his eyes, but at the same time there was something that looked like fear. While Charles sat by the stove Theodor walked back and forth in the cabin and inquired nervously about all his acquaintances up in the colony. Each time Charles stirred Theodor gave a start, then quickly went on with a sort of frightened entreaty in his voice. Charles didn't meet his eye; Theodor looked elsewhere. When Charles finally wanted to go, Theodor didn't try to hold him back. And then Charles went. But a few paces from the house he stopped with wide open eyes. A sort of smothered sobbing had sounded behind him. Charles stroked himself thoughtfully over his face and looked pensively at the closed door. Then he walked with muffled steps around the nearest hill, from which he came back whistling loudly and struck a blow on the door. It remained closed, and so he opened it himself. Just inside stood Theodor bent over. His eyes were forced wide open. It was as though a grass snake moved in his glance. When he saw Charles his expression changed, went from a grimace to a smile as he said, "Well, you've come back."

"Yes," said Charles and struck the sheath of his knife, "I've lost my knife."

They looked for it in the house, but it was nowhere to be found, and as their eyes met fleetingly, they saw through each other. Charles didn't mention the knife any more but sat down and spoke again.

He could stay for a while after all, he could just as well go later as sooner. However he had found an excuse to stay over a night in North Coulee. That man has belonged to death from his youth on, thought Charles. Ross Dane should have kept his fingers off him. But it was too much to ask for passivity in such a matter from the alive and dynamic King Dane who wasn't capable of acknowledging death and who for that very reason had become chieftain in Beaver Coulee. A faint smile went over Charles' face. Death, Ross had said, why should I care about that? It'll come of its own accord, I tell you, Charley!

- - -

Theodor thought about whether he should move away from the place. But if it wasn't in his nature to make war, it wasn't to his liking to give up, either. He couldn't leave the coulee in defeat, he had to stay there to the bitter end.

For him it wasn't a question of discussing what spirits were, whether they existed or not. He had lived among them for months and acknowledged them. For days he didn't go out of the cabin. If he were going to walk over the floor, he did so on the tips of his toes, but hour after hour he could sit stiff and bewitched in his chair, not daring to move his feet or chew his food. And the coyote knows the frightened human, it walks closer and sniffs while he moans in agony. If only he sensed one coyote, he saw before him the valley full of hairy shadow creatures with fire pricking out of their eyes.

When it happened that people came visiting, then their steps were on the point of killing him. With wild eyes he sat staring at the door until it opened, and he came back to life on seeing that the intruder was a person. But his shaken mind put a sinister look also into familiar people's features. He wasn't really capable any more of perceiving them as human beings - all right, as human beings, but what lay hidden under that word, was the word in itself not full of horror? Human features which habit had dulled the eye to were grasped by his glance as something hitherto unseen, and he understood that in life's every day a person is never seen as the demon it is, this upright walking creature on flat feet with forelimbs transformed into flapping, perverse grippers, and a face which is merely a collection of bold and aggressive sense organs. Even his friends, whenever he saw them, he came to regard as repellent - more than that, as emissaries from a world of darkness.

And the visits to North Coulee became rare. Rarer and rarer. In the colony to be sure they said that one really ought to go out and visit Theodor once in a while, but nothing more came of it. In the end no one came, and no one knew any longer how it was going with the hermit in North Coulee.

- - -

For a long time fear was over him only at night. One day he had been up at Ross's and had come back late. Night had fallen when he rode down into North Coulee and drove his horse over the obstacles in the bottom of the valley. It was as though someone spoke quietly in the glaring whiteness among the hills, and the feeling of dread captured him when from a hillslope he heard a spring whispering under the ice in the bottom of the valley where coyote tracks stood full of moon shadow. With a force as never before he experienced fear of the snow-laden hills, of the narrow valleys, the flat land and the distant slopes. Feeling as though he were covered with ice he came up to the cabin; half mad he took his horse along inside and tied it to the sleeping place. He lay with a hand on one of its legs to feel its company but then in the darkness began to imagine the horse's shape, the large body which was only carried - what secret powers had created the horse and what for? What was the horse? He dreaded that creature but didn't dare put it outside. Then he forgot it, for as he lay buried among the rags in the bottom of his sleeping box it happened that he saw the gable taken off the house, and he saw further out into the millennia-old coulee than he had ever done by the light of day. Far away on one of the white hillsides a child dragged itself forward through the deep snow. It came closer and closer, but became at the same time smaller until only a pair of large faded eyes were left. They remained hanging out there over the snow, keeping him prisoner until day broke. When the morning came the two staring eyes faded away in the daylight. The last remains of the vision disappeared, the house closed up again. Here are many spirits in the valley, thought Theodor, but anyway they are only one. And now I have seen the coulee's eyes.

From that time on the fear also came during the day. But he had to go out for meat, and it soon made no difference if he were outside or in.

Down in the valley was a lake with a little island covered with spruce trees. They curved up over the ice like the dome on a sunken church. Beside the bank stood a dead birch sharply drawn, reddened by the sunset. There was something so unreal about it that he imagined it was a rune written on the sky with a bloody finger.

A rabbit had been caught in one of his snares, but it had bitten through the branch the snare had been tied to and dragged it along. Round about the place the snow had been trodden into a depression with steep edges. Small branches had been bitten in two as if cut with a knife. Theodor stood looking at the traces of the little drama. Then he looked around. The sun had not yet gone down, the frost was hard, the snow shrieked wildly under his boots. Then in one of the trees a short way ahead he caught sight of a little spectacled owl. For a while he stood quietly to see it at closer range. Like a flake the bird floated over into another tree. He walked closer again. When he was almost as close as before, the bird didn't fly off but fell down into the snow at the foot of the tree and remained lying there. Theodor went over and looked at it. It was dead.

It made a strong impression on him. He knew well enough that birds too are mortal, but while he stood looking at the dead bird the thought came to him that this had never before in the world been seen by human eyes. And he mumbled to himself, "But I am also a gruesome breathing creature, I *am*, I live in North Coulee."

Up on the top of one of the smaller hills a strange formation attracted his attention, and he began with difficulty to work himself over the slope's crusted snow. About halfway up he could see that what stood on the hilltop was a random shape of earth, but since he had begun the climb he wanted to go all the way up anyhow.

Then something happened. Some power, not seen but all the more felt, wanted to force him back. It was almost as if a strong arm were laid on his chest from behind, and he noticed how cold he became. But whatever it was that occurred he didn't want to submit to it and continued upward. Soon it wasn't merely a physical force that acted on him but a psychological one as well, and a voice without sound spoke in his ear: Why don't you go back when you know that's best?

Drops of sweat suddenly began to fall twinkling down past his eyes, but he didn't want to give up. The voice spoke on in melancholy anger: Go back, go back.

Then he turned himself slowly around in the deep snow, not to go down but to strike. There was nothing to see. The world glittered everywhere in the coulee's snow, and it was as quiet as if there had never been life on the earth. But as he turned around he felt the struggle had ended. Whatever had been there withdrew, offended as it were: So then do what you want! He brushed his forehead with his sleeve and went upward again, but now very slowly. He had of course actually nothing to go up for, and his head buzzed with thoughts. Then he reached the top, but as he parted a bush, he stared down into an abyss. It was very deep, but not very wide, and almost looked as though the hill had once been split. He let himself fall into the bush and stared down, and he knew that if he had continued at his original speed he would now be lying dead at the bottom of the ravine. Down there in snow and stone scree lay the cadaver of a horse with a broken foreleg sticking white out of the skin. Three coyotes stood with lowered heads and upward turned eyes, small green window panes into fallen souls. Then they went into that stiff run which coyotes use in deep snow, a choppy pig gallop. They disappeared quickly in the ravine. A little later they appeared on a hill, they stood quiet and looked, the coyote always has to look. Their high, triangular ears were sharply outlined. Then they ran away. Theodor went down at once, but his knees were shaking. At the foot of the hill he fell in the snow and remained on his knees lying in snow to his waist several minutes while he thought about what had happened.

At last he got up and noticed, as though it were someone else who did so, that he smiled and said aloud, "The world is so big, so big."

But he was afraid of his own voice.

6.

That same fall before the snow came Ross took the car one Saturday and drove with his boys to town to recruit people. It was foggy and rainy, and because the threshing had been suspended there were many people in town. Moreover a dance had been planned at the hotel for the evening, although this was cancelled since the landlord had hanged himself - a great irritation to Ross Dane whom he owed money to, and to the young people who had turned out in strength.

Ross began at once to look for people, but didn't find any immediately. Then a vehicle came tearing along and stopped in front of the Chinaman's store. It was a new, elegant car of completely modern type with a large flat box on rubber tires tied to the back by a rod which was made fast under the car. When the car came to a halt things became lively under the blankets in the trailer. About a dozen men stuck their heads up from the box where they had been lying hidden under the blankets. One of them caught sight of Ross. He turned his chaw a couple of times in his mouth and asked, "What's the name of this town?"

Ross gave him the name and immediately wanted to recruit the whole gang. Nah, they were going to go further on! said the man, who jumped off the box and got bread and butter at the Chinaman's. He took it with him under the blankets in the box where the other men were lying stretched out beside one another, and then the car rushed out of town again like a comet with a tail of mud.

Ross looked after the comet with a broad grin. Damned if it hadn't been freethinker Jensen's terrified mug lying in the middle of the trailer. It looked like Jensen was still attaching himself to caravans on account of his great poverty.

A little later a farmer came to Ross and asked him to hire a couple of men who were sitting over at the Chinaman's. They were Danes, married people who were going to have their families sent for when they had collected enough money. Ross looked at them. Their names were Terkel and Hans, and they made a good impression, so Ross made an arrangement with them. They were to meet again in the evening.

When that had been attended to, Ross went off and made a deal on a threshing machine. It was an expensive affair, but he had got tired of the rented machines. One could never go by the weather and often missed good working days. Now he also counted on being able to earn money by renting out. That would surely be good business.

He let the boys go and walked around to say hello to people. On each of the four street corners stood groups in conversation, young men from many nations, gaily dressed up with leather down their pantlegs. Cowboys wobbled off on high heels, and tender prairie girls walked among bearded people in overalls. A fat Irishman dominated the whole street with his thick lips and showy cigar with band. In the middle of the crowd at the Chinaman's sat a newly washed lad licking icecream with his sweetheart. Reapers stood under the streetlight eating apples and smoking.

Somebody got a dance arranged in a loft, and it was so lively there that it thundered in the post office downstairs. Those who could dance kicked up their heels. Those who couldn't wrestled or walked on their hands. Clay jars with wine were passed around, and high spirits prevailed.

There Ross met with Eugen Huseby and told him about his threshing machine. "It's a fine machine, Huseby, and now you can rent it from me cheaper than from the old renters."

Huseby was quiet for a minute. "Then there will certainly be a hullabaloo again," he said. "Fyodor has bought a machine too. He has just asked if he might thresh for me. I told him some nonsense, but he probably thinks I've said yes."

Ross became irritated but didn't say anything. It was of course an honourable matter for Fyodor to buy a threshing machine. And Ross had first and foremost bought his for his own sake.

"But there will certainly be trouble," said Huseby, "for Fyodor will regard your purchase as a challenge."

Ross answered unmoved,

"Fyodor is a rat. I dare say he's come to learn that I'm a terrier."

Late in the evening Eugen Huseby's wife was insulted by the drunken Fyodor, and Huseby didn't let the punishment wait. He beat up Fyodor when he found him at the Chinaman's. Both window panes and table legs were destroyed. Ross gloated. There would probably be use for his threshing machine on Eugen Huseby's land after all!

Past midnight the cars scattered out into the prairie where rabbits couldn't find their way out of the headlights' beams, and where straw fires licked toward the sky.

- - -

After the brawl at the Chinaman's Huseby swore that he he wouldn't have anything more to do with Fyodor. It was Ross Dane who got his threshing. Several days after the threshing had been started on Huseby's fields a farm hand came over and warned Huseby. "I can't say anything definite," he said, "but Fyodor's going around like a devil who has the day off from Hell."

Huseby ignored this. However, toward evening the following day came Fyodor's revenge. The man who was throwing the sheaves into the threshing machine suddenly jumped back terrified in the wagon. With a furious noise the threshing machine came to a stop, the belt of the motor flew off, and then it was discovered what had happened: a steel rod had been stuck in the sheaf. Huseby didn't say much, but he was chalk white. Ross took his threshing machine home for repairs and afterward sent a farm hand to Huseby's with the message that he was not coming back. Then Huseby himself went over to his place to get an explanation.

"Surely you must be able to understand," said Ross, "that there's more than one iron rod in your sheaves. It can cost more than one threshing machine to continue."

They parted on bad terms.

The next night gunshots sounded, and the farmers locked their doors. The day after that it was made known that Fyodor's machine house had been burned down. At the last moment he had saved his threshing machine.

Many nights afterward people took care to stay inside. Everyone suspected everyone, and Ross Dane's new man Hans, who was inwardly convinced he ought to stay out of the whole thing, one evening got an ear ripped off by a rifle bullet. He was shaken. Shooting at people!

None of the parties summoned the police. They didn't trust lawyers and authorities. Fyodor now threshed on his own farm. He had dismissed all the northern Europeans and worked only with Galicians. Nevertheless somebody got at him. Suspiciously he had paced day and night by his threshing machine with rifle in hand, but one day he noticed there were noises in the machinery that shouldn't be there. He ground his teeth while he continued walking round and round to find the damage. Just as he was about to stop the machine it came to a stop by itself with a couple of gasping sounds. Fyodor flung down his rifle and, shaking, began to investigate the various parts. At last he stood with an off-screwed oil cup in his hand. With a flaming oath he threw it in over the field. It had been full of polishing powder. In a hurry he examined the others. There had been polishing powder in all of them.

Now Fyodor could no longer keep away from the authorities. With all the oil cups in a bag he rode in to the Polish lawyer, and a slow tug-of-war began there which ended at Christmas time without having come to any result. It wasn't a good idea to go anywhere near Fyodor. The lawyer had fleeced him thoroughly. Then he took up the war again single-handed. The Norwegian and Danish grain wagons on the way to the station had a weakness for overturning on the way, so one had to have an outrider with them to investigate whether the trail was safe. Livestock was found half-eaten by coyotes, horses disappeared. Just as that group of farmers who were outside the war, but to whom neither Huseby nor Fyodor paid much regard, had decided to complain to a higher authority, the war ended abruptly. Fyodor was found trampled to death by his own horses not far from his farm. That gave occasion for many rumours, but the police investigation led to nothing.

Afterward it meant dismissal if anyone mentioned the name Fyodor Murazezsky on Huseby's farm. Fyodor's widow continued working the property with the help of her eldest children. It was said she got support from Ivan.

Charles Villeneuve shook his head. People were precocious in Beaver Coulee. The first death, the first murder, blood, blood in human beings' tracks...

- - -

And his thoughts turned to another person in the colony. Death was already on the point of raising its scythe again. They had scoffed at the old reaper.

140

7.

Theodor walked slowly up the coulee slope with his rifle in one hand and the horse's reins in the other. His face was turned stiffly ahead, his movements completely automatic. He continued walking like this until he was in on the prairie. There he relaxed, and his eyes grew calm. Oh, thank God!

He jumped onto his horse and rode to Ross Dane's. It had been altogether necessary for him to see Eva today, and he became quiet when he was finally sitting in her kitchen, where the servant girls under her direction were preparing dinner for all of the many people. He thought he hadn't seen her for many years so like what she had been at that time long, long ago - almost a girl again, her eyes were so clear and mild. He thought it had to be a festive day and asked one of the servant girls about it. She became surprised. What was that supposed to mean, and why did he think that? Oh, he just thought... She looked around. She really couldn't see anything special. Theodor let it drop.

Later he sat alone reading. Then he heard Eva and Ross meet over in one of the sitting-rooms.

"You don't already regret the day after, Eva?"

She laughed. "No," she had thought it over properly in advance.

He too laughed softly. "Well, we'll see. Remember: Girls, and not fewer than three!"

Something sounded like a slap on a cheek, someone ran, a door slammed, there was noise outside.

A servant girl walked through the room.

"Ooh, how childish," she said. "Eva and Ross are having a snowball fight out on the veranda."

"Oh," said Theodor, tired.

He said goodby and rode over to Sigurd Huseby's. He was miserable. He tried to console himself: Eva was happy. Ah, poor comfort; he wished her not happy. He felt so homeless being among happy people. Now he wanted to ride over and ask Kaja to marry him. Her health would chase the evil spirits out of

North Coulee - yes, he was ready to take a nurse now, if she would take *him*.

Sigurd wasn't any friendlier than usual. And when Theodor was sitting again in the familiar room, he became sadder. He looked at Kaja, and he looked at Sigurd. Oh, if only he could die when he was ready, but then Ross Dane would stand in the way with his vitality and his aggressive, offensive health which tolerated nothing but health.

Theodor told her what he had come for, when they had been alone for a while.

She bent down and kissed him on the forehead.

"Have you thought it over long enough now, Theodor? Do you know what your name means? God's gift. He couldn't have given me anyone better."

"I'll give you the best I know," he said and took her hands, though he actually didn't like doing so.

She said she would like to go to North Coulee right away. They could easily be married - today she couldn't go with him, but tomorrow she would take the car and drive to North Coulee. And she whispered as Sigurd opened the door, "I'll stay out there."

She wasn't happy when he rode off. Something told her that there never could be anything good coming out of her relationship with   Theodor. When she saw him disappear among the hills she became very desolate. Sigurd stood with his rifle, fingering it covetously. He too looked out through the window pane after Theodor.

- - -

Theodor rode out to North Coulee in a state which was new for him. Everything future had happened, everything past returned, he had never lived until today and wouldn't live tomorrow, but life was an eternity.

His fear had been forgotten, but when he pulled up his horse on the last hilltop and looked out over the immense coulee, it broke out more violently than ever before. There stood a wall of cloud in the dark evening, becoming visible as the moon sent its light up over it. Then the full moon came all the way over the bank of clouds, the uppermost edge of which was a straight line. It was as if the moon went over a wall and tried to throw its light in on the prairie without however being able to drive away the billowing land's muddy darkness. The mountain-high coulee slopes on the opposite side stood like enormous expanses which had been raised on edge, their rims a wavy line against the sky. He got off his horse, could never sit on it going down into the valley. He turned away from the coulee and looked toward the red moon which had been stranded on one of the nearby hilltops. It attracted him, he had to go up there.

142

The snow shrieked under his leather boots, the air was full of screaming creatures. It led his thoughts into another direction. He stood still. Achingly the realization rose in him that this was madness. Slowly he went back to the slope. Tortured, he remained standing there while the horse drifted off down into the coulee. He knew that he would never go down. But neither could he turn his back again on that mysteriously breathing land which now month after month had robbed his soul. In a vision he saw himself both here and there in the valleys. They had taken him, and he had taken them. There was no way back. Kaja, it's too late, Eva, Eva, it's too late.

Eventually he sat down with his rifle over his knees and his index finger on the trigger, in defense, but never in attack, to the last. He bowed his head. A little later it began to snow. It snowed for an hour or so, and then the sky again became clear. The night passed.

- - -

The next day Kaja came as the first woman to North Coulee. She stopped the car where Theodor sat frozen in the snow. For a long time she sat looking at him from the car windows. When she slowly approached over the deep snow the tears broke out, becoming a chain of beads of ice down to the corners of her mouth. She didn't see that the rifle lay under the snow over Theodor's knees, and as she tried to break the frozen man loose, a cracking explosion echoed from hill to hill. She fell over him, lay a few seconds quietly, then slowly stretched one leg out, then the other one, and didn't move any more. Kaja, I gave you the best I knew.

The whole day the car stood humming, but at sunset it came to a stop with a couple of crude sounds. Again there fell a little snow. Toward morning three coyotes stood on a hill and looked down, but when it grew lighter they disappeared. The day came, it snowed a bit again, the two became a little hillock beside the car with snowdrifts on the roof and the radiator. The moon rose. That night several coyotes stood on the hills round about, but none came close. They closed the ring from night to night until the sixth one. Then a young coyote dug itself down and bit. It rushed off right away, flew off over the prairie, the others with it. But before the moon sank they stood in a circle shuffling their feet.

The seventh night they had forgotten their fear.

143

8.

When the funeral was over, Ross Dane stepped up to the grave and asked to be allowed to say a few words. Not concerning the sad thing that had happened, and about which people could neither know nor judge. But now here lay two graves. That meant church and pastor had been lacking until now in Beaver Coulee. It was virtually a Danish colony - "and look at our neighbours. Even though it's a long way to them, the Germans, the Galicians and the Norwegians, all of them have a church. When Fyodor died he was buried by and among his countrymen, beside his countrymen's church. I have thought a lot about our not having any church in Beaver Coulee, and what I want to say is that if all the adults of the colony will meet one day and designate five who will be in charge of the money for a church, then I'll pay the cost if others don't think they really have the means to go along."

No one answered. During the following days there was much discussion. In the end a deputation of three men called on Ross and delivered the message that no one liked the idea of using the money in that way. After all, they said, that was the money which the colony had been robbed of at the time Ross and Ivan had made a corner in wheat. They said Ivan's bad conscience had made him build a church with his share of the profit, but here people would find it more fitting if Ross let the money go back where it properly belonged.

Chalk white, Ross Dane heard them out. Then he was over them like a waterspout. He smashed two doors to bits with their bodies because in his rage he forgot to open them. He threw them out. He knocked them down again and again, kept after them, beating them until they were outside his barbed-wire fence.

Eva and the boys, dumbfounded, had watched the answer Ross Dane gave. Eva took a deep breath when he came in, and quietly walked away. Ross sat down. Quiet as mice the boys stood in a corner and stared at their father. His nostrils flared, his eyes were like a couple of lumps of liquid lead. Well, so those

145

devils would have poor relief established in Beaver Coulee! - They could come up here to King Dane one by one, they could, and get what-for. Ivan's bad conscience! He'd make them pale all right! - then he'd give them some good bright rainbow colours, those swine, skunks and maggots! Well, so they didn't want to have any church, no church! They would rather have his money and be without the word of God! He cursed and swore up and down. They would rather go and become freethinkers like that Jensen with his beard who had himself driven around in a trailer in order to make cuckolds of all the male coyotes in the quickest and cheapest way so that Beaver Coulee had some of the most beastly issue of huskies that had ever appeared on the American continent. Oh no sir! That sort of thing King Dane's money would not be used for. Well, so those good people didn't want to have any church? No? They'd get a church they had never dreamt the likes of. He had thought about spending $3000 to the glory of heaven; now he'd put aside $10,000. *He*, King Ross Dane of Beaver Coulee would build a church here on the highest hill, it would have both steeple and lightening rod, it would have an altar cloth with tassels, coloured pictures, and be inlaid with coloured chips and have the most beautiful arches. And then there would be a minister who knew the difference between Heaven and Hell, not one of those blockheads who imagined that Frederik Pedersen would get into heaven. The sermons would by God steam from that pulpit, and it would be elegant with carved cherubs and whatever else he could think of! They didn't want any church? Mangy freethinkers! He'd church them!

Suddenly he caught sight of the boys.

"Hey, are you standing there, Fred, Chris and Pete? Did you see me throw the freethinkers out?"

Yes, they had seen it. Oh father, how strong you are...

Ross laughed. "Well, there isn't a King Dane born every century, but all the same the Lord is going to grant that my powers be passed on. That's why he had the stork send me triplets, so all of you together can equal your father some time. Heigh ho."

With a calm grin he set about rolling a cigarette. The triplets recognized that look and pressed him at once for a quarter each. Eva came in and looked at him for a long time. He answered with the continuing grin and rubbed his nose thoughtfully.

"Ross, you should bear in mind that we are no longer living completely in the old wild days. The boys take after you. And it's no thanks to you that those three men got away from the farm alive. You're playing with our existence."

Ross Dane got up and kissed his wife. "Eva, queen of Beaver Coulee, don't get mixed up in affairs of state. Damn it, it's hard enough already when you're supposed to be king and army both."

146

Over at Pedersen's farm a dozen or so men had been standing looking for the deputation. They spoke respectfully about the grand air with which it had moved inside for an audience. But when it came out, Frederik was frothing at the mouth. With a lot of onlookers' heads all trying to get a look at the same time, a windowpane was knocked out. But old Pedersen couldn't stand for such a sight. To be sure he was on bad terms with Ross, but in his heart he considered Frederik and the others lunkheads that they didn't want to have a church given to them. And it was so beautiful to see those three men get a beating - and regardless of the reasons. He grasped his beard with both hands, opened his mouth like a sea devil and laughed so that his stomach bounced. It was good for a weary heart! Ho, ho, hoo, hee - hah, hoh, heh, hey! Oh! Oh-hooo! God help me that's how guests go home from Ross Dane!

Frederik ran over furiously and gave his father a slap. Pedersen stopped abruptly, shocked. Some gentleman, heh, clout his old father. That was the thanks you got for bringing up children in the nurture and admonition of the Lord. Then he remembered the chucking-out scene and went over into his barn to get the grin off his face in peace. Heh, heh, that Ross! Throw out people like carrots! *That* was the kind of son one should have had, and not one who beat his father, or one who ran off with his money, shot women with a rifle and died of God knows what. Heh, heh, that Ross, there was good stuff in him.

- - -

One of the men whom Ross had hired in town, Hans, at first had not lived up to the demands ordinarily made of a worker on the prairie, and these weren't reduced at Ross Dane's. But he had happened to see how Ross got rid of unwelcome guests, and that had changed him completely. Now things started to get done. He licked Ross's boots and chopped wood for Eva. He's like a dog, thought Ross. Best to get rid of him again.

Terkel was of another sort - not an especially good worker, somewhat delicate, but steady. He never started hurrying just because Ross appeared, but he didn't slacken off either whenever Ross left. Besides, Ross had seen The New Testament in his baggage, and that meant a good deal at a time when Ross Dane saw himself surrounded by rotten freethinkers everywhere. And just look, on getting his first wages Hans went off and bought himself a scarf, some sort of trash for decoration, but what did Terkel do? He said, "If you're going to town, Ross, then send half of the money to my wife and put the rest in the bank. You can keep on doing that, but slip me twenty-five cents a week for chewing tobacco."

That Terkel was a peach of fellow and if he continued developing that way,

147

damn it he'd give him a loan for a ticket. It was a tough thing having one's Eva on the other side of an ocean, yes. Ross sighed. He'd been through that once, even though there hadn't been any separating ocean. Actually that must be worse - but then things were different now.

Ross smiled. Indeed. Terkel would have a ticket for his Eva.

And Ross saddled his horse and took a ride, just for the fun of it. He nodded up at the sun, smiled, yes, indeed, an excellent world for people who weren't freethinkers and who had their fists properly screwed on their arms.

He rode out and had a pleasant chat with old Ivan, the Galician with the low, broad forehead and the steady, mild eyes. "I had thought for that matter that we ought to make a new corner in wheat, Ivan, for it was getting somewhat monotonous around here, but then came that church business, and so we'd best wait till another time. What fools! They don't want to have a church. Well, I'll build one anyway and engage a minister for me, Eva and the triplets. There aren't going to be any freethinkers in my family. And you can bet, Ivan, that I understand about the ungodly. When the church is there, they'll want a share too in the heavenly roast lamb. It's no use for example my going over into your church. You have such queer customs there that it makes it uncomfortable for me, and besides the priest speaks Galician with God. I can't help believing he likes Danish better."

Ivan nodded.

"That he does - when he is surrounded by Danes."

Ross became thoughtful. What would it come to in the long run in these vast lands? The Germans built churches on the prairie and heard their own language, the Dutch did the same, and Galicians, Swedes, Norwegians. It was a downright return to Babylon.

The rumour spread right away that Ross Dane wanted to build a church on his own and as it suited him. First there was a flare-up: He absolutely didn't have a right to! But then if you thought it over - this was Canada and not Denmark - and over there in Denmark for that matter couldn't anyone build a church if it suited him? Still one didn't just do it like that out of hand. To be sure Ross Dane could cover his whole farm with churches if it fitted in with his purse, and engage a minister in each one! And now if he built one, so what? Then it stood there. But it was going to be built with *their* money, dishonest mammon.

"Now, now, a church is a church," said Pedersen.

And he was right enough after all. A church was a church. Baptisms, weddings and that sort of thing - no, it just wouldn't be an easy matter at all, and then of course they'd actually paid for the whole thing themselves...

As for Ross, when he had quieted down, Eva asked him to wait with that

148

church. Naturally he should build it. But the colony should have a voice. He knew very well who stood behind the resistance - it was Frederik - and she had heard from the women that many people were annoyed at Frederik and found the whole thing hasty. A church shouldn't be a slap in the face. It was *he* who was ungodly.

Ross stared at her. *He!* And she got the whole lesson about freethinkers, coyotes, Frederik, Jensen, Hans with the scarf, and his own, Ross Dane's, indescribable piety.

But Eva parted his hair with her hands, pulled his ears a bit - and Ross Dane put off his church building.

9.

Hans began to notice Ivan's daughter. She was very pretty, lovely as a tiger cub. But - she was of course Galician. Hans didn't consider that. He hadn't lived long enough in the country to be indoctrinated with such prejudices. Ivan discovered that Hans was laying himself out to please and enlightened his daughter about two things: namely, that Hans belonged to the (with rare exceptions) inferior Nordic race, and that he was married as well. The first he impressed on her with philosophy, the latter with a birch rod.

But that of course didn't have much effect on Hans, who had got neither philosophy nor a thrashing. And the girl liked him. A thrashing she got anyway now and then for the sake of health and decency, and philosophy didn't have a permanent residence in her little heart where there was only room for passion.

Then Ivan chose to go up and speak with Ross. Pedersen was standing at his window. Heh, heh, in a short while one would see that little Hans came down into the bottom of the coulee on his head, for now the prime minister was going to the king to report the decline of morals in sunny Alberta!

But Pedersen's expectations were upset. For Hans was of course not a stranger who came into a man's preserves and called him a swindler. Hans was in Ross Dane's employ, and what he had done didn't concern Ross. Other means had to be resorted to.

Ross went out into the barn to Hans and asked him if he weren't married. Hans glowered. Yes, he was. And his wife was coming to Canada? Yes, of course. Who the devil did he think he was, wanting to ruin a young girl?

Hans looked helplessly about. He was very much afraid of Ross Dane. But he mumbled anyway that such a thing was certainly a private matter - that is as far as he knew.

"Well, but it's wrong, you see," said Ross. "Now I'll make you a proposal. First I will tell you that I have never broken a promise - except once, and that was to a man I promised to shave. He was sick, you see, but when I came he was dead, and so it didn't matter. On the other hand I have never countenanced

151

anyone's giving me empty promises. Will you promise me not to go near Ivan's daughter or in any way get in contact with her?"

Ross Dane's calmness made Hans shake. Ordinarily Ross was quick in his turn of speech. Even a pleasantness came out like a shot of water in the face. But Hans managed then with chattering teeth to say that he with pl-pleasure would look for another job if Ross weren't satisfied with him.

"By all means," said Ross. "But there's this promise now."

Hans looked out of the corner of his eye at Ross who had sat down on a box and was rolling a cigarette. Like a rocket Hans rushed to the door. But in the middle of his wild race he was surprised - Ross didn't move. At the doorway he was taken by the neck and the seat of his pants and thrown back in. Then Ivan closed the door from the outside to avoid more inconvenience.

"Come here," said Ross, as he let his lip go over onto the cigarette paper's gummed edge.

But Hans' nerves couldn't take any more. He couldn't give in, but his fear made him crazy. Half in convulsive sobbing he cried out, howled and cried, shouted something about scoundrels, assault, cruelty, slavery. Ross smoked his cigarette and didn't look at him at all. Finally Hans became silent. Out of the corner of his eyes he observed Ross.

"Come on."

Slowly Hans walked a few paces until the distance between them was the same as before.

"The promise," said Ross.

Hans didn't answer.

"You certainly know of the story about a spanking that Frederik Pedersen got," said Ross slowly. "I had put $1000 aside for it, and I was only going to have a little revenge. I saved $300. If I put a similar value on you, in other words $1000 plus the $300 I saved with interest... Say no, little Hans, then you'll earn a couple of hundred dollars. As regards those $1300 I won't be so particular about them. You may have a beating for $3000. Then of course I'd have to use an iron chain..."

If Hans didn't answer it was probably because he couldn't.

"It's like this you see," said Ross thoughtfully. "Ivan is my friend. I'd bring him your head in a sack if he wanted it. But he doesn't want that, for Ivan is a peace-loving man who doesn't collect heads, especially your kind. Well, people like Ivan - it would be a good thing for the world if there were more of them. I'm sitting here wondering if I couldn't really spend $4000 for his sake. But then I'd have to use a double iron chain, and I'd very likely be too tired to manage all that at one time."

Hans staggered a bit. Then he fell. Ross stared in astonishment, took his hat off and scratched the back of his neck. Slowly he began to comprehend. He thought deeply and for a long time while Hans lay unconscious. The king of Beaver Coulee - that was a by-name Fyodor had once created, and Ross had laughed and accepted it. It amused him. And Fyodor grew furious. For the name became a title. But now Ross suddenly realized that obviously it would never have become anything more than a by-name without some justification. He knew naturally that he was a man to be reckoned with, that he wasn't a non-entity among people. He had become strong here, yet had never consciously striven for power.

Today - he looked around as though he were waking up - his power was so great, and he so famous, that he could play with a grown man like a cat with a mouse, scaring the life out of him with words of which he didn't mean a fraction.

Hans came round. "Ross, Ross, I'll never, never so much as look at her...do you hear, Ross..."

Ross Dane looked away.

"No tricks with other ones either, and see to getting your wife over here as soon as you can," he said sternly. "If you get down to work, then you can count on getting help from me. We won't talk about this any more."

Hans and Ross got on well afterward. But now people noticed that the smile left Ross Dane's face whenever he was called the king. He never used the name any more himself, and his strong arms had been raised for the last time in violence when he kicked the church deputation out. But it wasn't said aloud that the king's army had been sent to its quarters. Ross was too sensible to do that.

Hans sat every Saturday evening writing a letter to his wife. You must forgive me, he wrote, for writing so little at first, but everything was so new here, and I had to get used to many things that were completely unknown in Denmark. I have been exaggerating in those few letters I sent. It isn't so bad with animals and such here, I only thought so when I first came. People live here just as safely as in Jutland.

It was hard for Hans to get it put together. After having met Ivan's daughter, he had begun to send home dramatic descriptions of the animal life in Canada. Ah, well, Hans sighed. It had seemed so innocent, but he didn't hide from himself now what his idea had been. Hans' interest in zoology had appeared rather recently, and he had entirely lost it again now. At home in Denmark a timid woman had sat shaking with fear whenever she read his letters. The horror of a prairie which she had never seen had grown in her. With each letter her fear became greater. Hans was not at all happy about this now and sweated over the difficult problem of explaining away not only his own letters but the

153

whole animal kingdom of Canada.

His fear of Ross became idolization. Everything Ross did was right and perfect. The hardest thing to comprehend was Ross's monogamy. Why it was not at all modern; Ross was a relic of the past. Hans was deeply rooted in the interpretations of love of his own fashion and age level. He had come to Canada with his brain overgrown with naive ideas of polytechnic polygamy, the right of love and all the sort of thing that oozes in a mind that hasn't known love yet.

But he learned well. At last he had only one great sorrow, and that was that his dear wife's name was Nicoline. If only she had another name! He was on the verge of tears whenever Ross told his hair-raising stories about freethinker Jensen, for then Nicoline always emerged as a symbol of everything rotten in the world. In the long run Hans could not take it. He sneaked in to Eva one day, mumbling a lot of strange things. She couldn't make out what it was, pushed him down into a chair - so, let's hear it! Red in the face, he stammered, "Oh, it's just Ross and then Nicoline..."

"Well?"

"Well, you see...that's my wife's name, you know."

Eva sent Hans away, but it was too much to demand of Ross that he should be quiet about Nicoline's obscenity. He agreed to give her a change of name, however. She got the name Rasmine. Then Hans was consoled.

10.

Charles had been away for a long time. It was fall when he came home from horse dealing in the East and at Ross Dane's heard about Theodor's death. Ross was not at all eager to tell him about it. He looked furtively at his old friend all the while. Charles was tactful, just made a remark about death striking blindly. He had his own views. Blindly? Oh, no, the old reaper had wide-open eyes.

Then they talked about other things. Yes, Charles had made a pretty penny this time. Moreover it was strange to see how things were growing on the prairie now. The whole way through Manitoba and Saskatchewan he had seen farms, binders were going. Out here you could always see the smoke of the threshing machines, and the straw fires blazing. Yes, they were new times. Ross should take a trip east and see. A prairie fire of the old-fashioned kind was not conceivable any more. But Ross Dane shook his head. No, he was needed here. The farm was being transformed into a large scale concern. It was more and more demanding. And Charles stole a glance at Eva. Ross certainly didn't go far from his farm these days; otherwise Charles would have thought of taking him along out to his own threshing - it was in full swing when he came home.

He rode off alone. Ross sat looking sadly after him. Charles was not happy. His children, two sons and two daughters, weren't like their father. The two daughters - they could have used some of the candy Ivan's daughter was born with. But otherwise one didn't hear much about them. Both inside and out they were Indian, had jet black hair, dwarf ears, copper brown skin and stormy features. They had the Indian's animal look and kept to the redmen who came down to Charles's from the forests. Like their mother they harboured hostile feelings toward the white men. In the sons, a couple of youngsters in puberty, only the strangely fluid, greenish look in their eyes betrayed their Indian blood. They were animal eyes, but yet the look was more coldly deliberate than in white men, calm, far-seeing, knowing. They were the eyes of the prairie people

155

and made a white man think about all the animals of the land, the lynx, the coyote, the eagle and the old moose.

The boys were hated in Beaver Coulee. They stole. They couldn't speak the truth. People put their finger on the trigger whenever they met William and Barni in out-of-the-way places. Why didn't Charles do anything? Presumably he would have been able to manage them if he had wanted to. But it didn't seem that Charles wanted to. He gave his sons a wistful look at times. He never reprimanded them. They were regarded as a kind of animal that resembles humans and is protected all year round, a beast of prey equipped with hands and human shrewdness. But they were frequent guests at Pedersen's, and it was known they were sweethearts with his daughters.

Mette and Else, still not full-grown, had never come to be like other girls in the colony - they were strayed human beings just as one had strayed horses. They hadn't the corrupt look of fallen women of culture; they were neither fallen nor sinful. They were wild. Whenever Ross saw them he instinctively thought of a lasso. "Heh, heh, those injuns," said Pedersen whenever William and Barni came. But he looked helplessly at them. He was afraid of the foreign blood, and suffered from an indeterminate fear whenever the two were on his farm. When both Mette and Else began sewing children's clothes, Pedersen looked around weakly - well, what will be will be. Frederik neither said nor did anything. The girls didn't interest him.

One fine day one of them disappeared with William. The other went around alone for a week, then Barni fetched her. Pedersen scarcely noticed that the girls were gone. It was said in the colony that William and Barni had exchanged sweethearts before they got married. Mette was asked about this once when she came south on a visit to Beaver Coulee. She said it wasn't true, for Else and she hadn't been sweethearts with one specific brother, but could of course marry only one. "Heh, heh," said Pedersen. He would rather not talk about the affair. Anyhow now Else and Mette were provided for, and apparently they were contented. So what? They had got men after their own hearts. And Pedersen insisted on the right of the heart since it had got Else and Mette several hundred miles out of the way. It was a good thing with such a heart. Pedersen had gradually come to feel for the girls as if they were two wandering flames among the wooden houses. He became composed again now. If Else and Mette couldn't get on with their husbands they would presumably find themselves other ones. They looked healthy. The inheritance - well, fortunately he could leave it to Frederik to bicker with them about. Heh, heh, there would certainly be a fine hullabaloo with those injuns one day when he kicked the bucket, heh, heh! In time you'll certainly get something else to think about besides cursing Ross, little Frederik.

Ross laughed broadly when he heard about the girls' marriage. "It's exactly like in the old days when Nico... I mean, when Rasmine was here. And the people, they're no better nowadays than the coyotes were in the old days. White girls running around on the prairie at night until they go completely to the injuns...mind you real injuns, not those who are only called that, like that Charles."

But Ross was sad. He felt sorry for Charles, the red man with the white heart, the warrior Charles who had joined the race he thought doomed to death.

It was clear that Charles despised his kin. There wasn't hate in his eyes whenever he looked at his children, but he simply held them in contempt. Yet one took care not to talk to him about his family affairs. In every way one had respect for Charles. He was a real white man.

A steady worker Charles was not. When other farmers were directing the work at their threshing machines, Charles was satisfied with a short visit now and then. Almost always he was hunting, on foot or on horseback. And during trips to the East his wife took over completely the running of the farm. The whites did not understand him. In particular it irritated some of them that he could let somebody else take the wheel when it was a matter of such importance as threshing. Now when Charles came riding up to his threshing machine one of the Danish farmers stood there with a sarcastic remark about people who in the busy season could ride around in a fancy uniform. Charles turned his horse and stared at the Dane, who became small under the Metis's look. Then Charles slowly lifted his rifle, let it point at the farmer's head and said, "You Danish man, who talks so much, you will jump twelve times over that ditch there and twelve times back."

The farmer became pale, and he hesitated. But then he went over and began jumping.

Had the order come from a white man he would scarcely have obeyed. But it was known for certain that one could depend on what Charles promised - and his look promised a rifle bullet...

This sort of thing Charles seldom did. He put up with much for the sake of peace. But sometimes chords in his mind could sound with a peculiar ring. Never could he run away from the fact that half of his noble ancestors belonged to the red prairie people.

Only Ross Dane could call him his friend. Though Charles's farm gradually came to lie in the midst of a colony of northern Europeans, mostly Danes, increasingly in the course of time he preferred the red race. And he became still quieter than before. Indians came wandering down to his place. He hunted with them and helped them in dealing with the furtraders.

- - -

Hans wanted to be friendly with Terkel. But Terkel was suspicious, he had never liked Hans, and it struck him that on Ross Dane's farm there had been more joy over the converted than over the righteous one who hadn't needed conversion. Terkel minded his own business and didn't intimate that he noticed Hans's overtures. Terkel wasn't completely the same as when he had come, either. A new world couldn't change him as long as he made his living and had his wife. The latter he didn't have, though, and it made him gloomy.

What kind of women were there here? They didn't look like being able to do much work, and he never overcame his distrust of these blonde, graceful creatures who didn't know anything about being shy and who came riding up to Ross's in men's clothes or drove a car. He didn't believe in them. There had to be something false somewhere. They walked around in patent-leather shoes on week-days and talked too much to people they didn't know. Such a girl could drive to town one day and come home with a new hat without her parents' being asked. Was it perhaps not with *their* own money? Terkel scowled at seeing that kind of thing. Look now at Ivan's daughter, dressed so that it was downright disgusting. It reminded him of that day in Copenhagen when he was over getting a ticket. All the ladies were dressed in such a way that it was clear they never did any work. They weren't a bit ashamed. The whole world realized they weren't blocks of wood gliding off on the edge of a skirt. He felt indignant. And here it ought to be different, for they were living in the country and should have more of an idea of decency. Obviously they didn't. Then Terkel was also indignant at people who didn't speak Danish. It was all right with the Canadians themselves. But Ivan, Huseby and all the others - Terkel wasn't completely clear, but he felt it was an insult against good form that they spoke so affectedly. He became embarrassed hearing them speak. They could at any rate lower their voices a bit and not display their lack of manners to that extent, but such pompous asses probably went around thinking themselves somebody. He was glad he was another kind of person and knew what was proper. It had been the same in Copenhagen - they had also spoken loudly to each other there without considering whether there were strangers in the room. Just snootiness, all of it.

Terkel felt no urge to turn the world from the way of sin. It wasn't worth it. There wasn't anybody to preach to either. He despised Hans. And the others who at that moment were on the farm didn't speak Danish - except for Ross himself and he couldn't really be included, for he went around in a constant state of unrest. An increase in the family was expected.

The day it happened there were both a doctor and nurse at the farm - in addition to a horde of women. Ross became the little one compared with such a great superior force. They chased him out though he maintained he had more experience and understanding in this than all the women together. He hung around agitatedly with vacant eyes until he was called toward evening.

The baby was a boy - and only one.

A shadow passed over his face. The boy should have been a girl. But he forgot it almost at once. For it *was* then a boy.

"That's one side of the undertaking which must be entrusted to the Lord," he declared. "And a girl can of course be wonderful, but a boy, anyway it is a boy now! And he's going to be named Charles Villeneuve Dane, for that I have promised, and it's also a nice name, and we must remember of course to give him one good enough for him when he takes office as Governor General!"

- - -

When Hans came in and saw the newborn, he stood for a long time silently, with an expression different from any he had ever been seen with before. Later he almost asserted a right of ownership and developed into a splendid babysitter. For some time he became more reserved than Terkel. For Hans had a child in Denmark; it had been only a few months old when he left. I wonder what that little creature looks like now...?

Then he went to Ross and asked for a loan. He got it, but Ross also wanted to help Terkel since he was in the same situation. Terkel answered no thanks, he didn't want to incur debts. A bit offended, Ross answered that he surely hadn't thought of charging interest. No, but even so, answered Terkel glumly, there existed so much irresponsibility, and he wanted to avoid that.

Ross didn't really understand him. It was surely both cheapest and best...and everything considered...well, it was up to Terkel of course. Ross was hurt. He felt a sort of reprimand in Terkel's refusal. Perhaps that man really belonged over on the other side of the coulee with Pedersen and his crowd. Ross didn't know what lay behind the words. Terkel knew that Hans had got a loan. What might *he* get now? Lord, I have borne the day's trouble and heat, while this other one...no, he would rather do without. Then he wouldn't owe any thanks to Ross Dane either.

- - -

In the spring Hans went to meet his wife in town. It was a warm day. Since Hans didn't drive a car, he borrowed Ross's light Democrat. He drove alone. Though he left in good time he became nervous on the way and reached town in a furious trot an hour before time.

On the farm a spread awaited them. It became one o'clock, and Eva peered out: Now they should soon be here. When it was two o'clock, they were afraid something might have happened with the train or the buggy. It became three o'clock. Then they didn't talk any more about what could be keeping Hans. The boys asked if they shouldn't ride toward town and see. No, said Ross curtly.

At the station the two couldn't really say anything; they only said hello. The little child had been sick in the train, but was sleeping now. Later they sat silent beside each other on the buggy on the way out to Beaver Coulee.

There stood a little gray wooden house in the tall grass. "What is that?" she asked timidly. "It's a grainary, sort of a storage place for grain," said Hans. "We put the grain in there from the threshing machine and sled it later to town... You can see it..."

He pulled up the horses and helped her down. She was carrying the child, and he put his arm about her shoulders. The door closed so irrevocably behind them, it was as if it had never been opened.

The horses walked away grazing while the day passed and the shadows became long. Then Hans came out and walked off to get the wagon. She stood in the door and looked calmly after him. Such was the prairie, very different from Denmark, but then it was earth with a sky above. And Hans was good, he had worked and saved for her sake. It was probably good that he had come to another country. She sighed and was contented. He was very changed, so smooth in his speech, no scowl at all in his glance.

11.

Ross went out on a long trip, the longest he had made since coming to Alberta. He discovered he was known at places far from Beaver Coulee, and not always for his virtues. He bled the poor white by making them dependent. He bought land and sold it at exorbitant prices to his countrymen. He was a tyrant to his people, he beat his wife and had murdered a Galician. Ross was a little perplexed, but brushed the feeling quickly aside - he was out on serious business. When he eventually came home, it was completely clear to him what three or four different types of church cost, how one got hold of and paid a minister, and a lot more. Eva had to write many letters for some time after this, and the colony realized that Ross had not given up his plans for a church. But the summer passed and nothing happened. More time passed, still nothing new. So Ross had probably given up his daring idea after all.

But Ross hadn't given up anything. It was just that there was so much new to occupy his thoughts. Now there were hundreds of young Danes who each summer appeared in Beaver Coulee, and he had always been inclined to think there were too many. A flood of people poured in over the country. Now came the masses. In the old days it was only the hard-bitten ones who had sought out these regions, but now came farmers, brush-makers and bookkeepers one after the other. The excess of all classes from the old world were going to earn gold in this country.

- - -

Ross dreaded letting the boys go. They had lived here under his eyes for so many years now, and they were turning out as he wished. He looked from them to Eva. All three of them resembled her through and through. The little one did so too. A painful joy shone in his eyes. It was good luck for a boy to resemble his mother. And he himself was also a lucky man. Shame on him if he said anything different. But it was without joy that he gave in to Eva's wish that the boys should study. He tried to soften the matter now that it was ultimately going to be that way. Was not everybody a farmer in one sense or another? And what if the boys now became so in a better way than he? But then Ross smiled tolerantly at his own thoughts. Naturally the triplets couldn't be greater farmers if they left the farm, however much, as engineers or whatever it might be, they subjugated the earth. The strange thing was that the boys themselves wanted to get away from Beaver Coulee. That was what Ross understood least of all...

He walked out onto his veranda and stood listening out toward the dark, where the coyote in the distance cried so bitterly because those nasty rabbits wouldn't let themselves be eaten tonight. Ross came to realize what the sounds of the prairie meant to him and that he would never be able to do without them. They were for the ear what the coulee and the billowing fields were for the eye.

His thoughts went far back. He saw himself wandering about like a tramp down in the northern States. Why had he done that? Probably just because... Well, he had never thought about it, not then either. Now it was impossible to think of leaving Beaver Coulee. But the boys - with them it was probably the same as with him when he left his home in South Dakota - and never came back. If only one could guide them a bit. But he thought about his own youth: No, they certainly wouldn't let themselves be guided. At least, though, they would be within reach of his arm and thoughts if they went to school...and Ross turned around quickly, went in and said to Eva that everything considered it was very likely a good idea about that schooling. "I have thought it over now. It's only been that I think a bit more slowly than you do, Eva. Of course they must leave us, and that is the best way. I did it on my own and differently when I was a boy, but it was a lottery from day to day, so that it's a wonder that I am sitting alive and safe now in Beaver Coulee. I don't begrudge the lads a better youth, fewer blows of all kinds - and more joys. Let them go. I must continue here where I was placed, and you must too. They shall go out... Yes, they shall...for they want to. I'm continuing right here on this spot... That church, Eva, we're going to have it erected. I dare say it's just as important that we go on building as it is that the lads leave and get a start."

Eva didn't look up. She was contented. Ross had given in, he was still the wisest, he always realized she was right. Not everyone could pride themselves on having so sensible a husband.

- - - -

Jens, that Danish immigrant who had left his family to look for work, never

162

came back. So much can happen in a large and foreign country. Jens hadn't spoken English at that time, and this hadn't made things easier for him. Now everyone gossiped about Sigurd Huseby's calling regularly on Jens's wife, and Ross Dane offered her and her children shelter if she wanted to have it at his place. She said no. There was nothing to be done about it; she was presumably satisfied with Huseby. And at last she moved with her children up to Sigurd's farm. It was seldom mentioned that they weren't married. The woman was of course in a bad position.

- - -

Life ran its course in Beaver Coulee. One struggled through the seasons, taking the cuts and bruises which came with existence. Fixed frameworks formed around society. Emigrants were no longer so welcome as before - they were now viewed as people outside the local community who were not as closely connected. Expansion of the population was one's own responsibility. Those who had a desire to build a world up from the bottom set out for some other area on the prairie. Ross Dane's own sons came home from college and trained themselves for work again. Ross smiled. The books hadn't spoiled the triplets. But he wasn't their master any more. In a couple of months each of them came home with a sweetheart and began consulting together out in the barn as they had done in the old days. Ross suspected change, he walked around and was uneasy. What would happen? Whatever it might be, he hoped at any rate that the three wouldn't deprive Eva and him of the youngest, Charles, the pledge on a love that could never die.

But when all four of them came to say they wanted to go up and farm in the new lands around Peace River, then Ross Dane fell silent. He was aging a bit, but remembered his own parents clearly now. They hadn't been happy when the children flew out of the nest. He himself, Ross, they had never seen again. He had only come back to look at graves.

Eva cried a little secretly, and Ross became more silent. But the sons set out with their share of the inheritance from Beaver Coulee. They had big dreams. Well, well, little Eva, they want a whole lot, but they will just come to live our own life over again. Can we wish them more, Eva?

12.

Pedersen was imperishable. Ross couldn't see that he had changed since coming to Alberta, though now he was over seventy. Animosity still continued between the two farms, but it led a subterranean existence and no longer sent branches out into the rest of the colony.

Since his sons had left, though, Ross Dane set aside old hate. The church was to be erected. He would rather pay for it and build it himself - then it would be as it should be. But Eva - she said of course no, the church should be built by the colony. And look, Ross, there would have been a church here many years ago if you hadn't been here.

He chewed on that a bit. I dare say she is right...

One day when Ross figured that most of the farmers could not be at absolutely necessary work, he saddled his horse and rode around to them. At the first farm he set forth a plan: They had to have a church in Beaver Coulee. Everyone wanted it of course. He would gladly refrain from contributing if that was the way it was going to be. But the church ought to be erected, and only bickering had prevented this from happening long ago. Now everyone should give, even if it were only a little, all the way down to ten cents. He himself had started the collection with a dollar. He would certainly be allowed to contribute that much at any rate. He would add three thousand if it was desired. One of the usual wooden churches, he had thought.

He was at the home of the colony's poorest man, but the latter gave ten dollars. Then Ross asked him to accompany him, and they rode off at once. They could not allow themselves to be delayed if they were going to get around in a day, and good horses were necessary.

Late in the afternoon a mighty procession passed through Beaver Coulee on the way to Pedersen's farm. Frederik was standing outside with wrinkled brows. He saw almost all the families of the colony represented in this army. All the Norwegians were there except Sigurd Huseby. The German and the Dutchman were there too. But no Galicians... Frederik knew very well that there was something happening today, but he had not wanted to ride out to ask. Now here was the whole colony - except the Catholics and the Methodists. Then it must be a matter of the church. See how unpretentious Ross Dane had become. He was among the last.

Pedersen had been standing behind the window pane, his lips quivering. When the crowd of people rode up to the farm he appeared in the doorway. At the bottom of his heart was a bit of fear. Why were all these men coming? There was Eugen Huseby, worth $75,000, Ross Dane at least double that, Peter Hansen, $20,000, Jens Frederiksen, $50,000, Sorensen, nothing...

"Heh, heh, so here comes King Dane with his legions," he said and stroked his beard. His eyes wandered uneasily.

Ross rode over to him.

"The reason we're coming to you last, Pedersen, is only because your farm is situated where it is. We had to go around the whole circle today, you see. Also this way you've avoided riding around. All the people you see here have given money to our church. Will you join in?"

Pedersen looked furtively at Frederik. But when he looked at Ross Dane he stiffened.

"Well then, hm - how much?"

"As you like, Pedersen."

"Heh, heh, what are you giving yourself?"

"That you can decide."

"Heh, heh..."

Pedersen was in distress. Frederik began to speak.

"What do you mean by that, Ross?"

"I mean that if you don't want to have me along, then it doesn't matter. You'll let me give a dollar anyway. But if I may share the risk, then I'll pay three thousand."

"What do the others say?"

"Well, we weren't going to say anything until you've given an answer."

"You say that if we agree you're to join in you'll pay three thousand?"

Ross kept a straight face.

"Do you want to join in?" he asked

"Yes," answered Frederik, "and we want - like the others! - to see you included."

Then Ross laughed.

"Damn it, it didn't work out. A fine mess! Three thousand right out of my pocket... How much are you giving?"

"Heh, heh..." said Pedersen.

"Is that all?" asked Ross seriously.

The whole crowd laughed.

"Heh, heh..." Pedersen looked around uneasily. "We could of course talk..."

"Oh, we don't need to talk," said Frederik, his voice cutting. "We'll give the same as Ross Dane. And hereafter there'll be peace in Beaver Coulee!"

It had become quite still. Old Pedersen was rocking back and forth. "Heh, heh. That..t...bah...heh...ba..."

It was as if a large slice had been cut out of him. He felt altogether airy. There were tears in his eyes. What hellish luck he had with his sons...

Frederik went on:

"You know, Ross Dane, that sort of thing is difficult. But I say again: Let's keep the peace. I will never come to like you, I think you're an oaf and a bandit. But from now on let us keep the peace. If I break it, I'll pay three thousand more..."

"Done! Same here."

Ross bent down and gave Frederik his hand. Pedersen finally recovered. Three thousand dollars! But then of course that placed one up beside Ross Dane. Dear me, dear me, had Frederik become stark raving mad?... Three thousand dollars...but that was spilled milk, it couldn't be lapped up. Pedersen mechanically stuck out his tongue at the thought.

"Now we have Pedersen sticking his tongue out at himself," grinned Ross. "Frederik, does our wager apply to him too?"

Aghast, Pedersen drew in his tongue: "Heh, heh, my good Ross, it's nice to have tolerance again between us old-timers. Heh, heh, little Frederik, can you remember the time the prairie burned up in Saskatchewan while we sat in a mud-hole on top of that Jensen? Heh, heh, that Jensen! And to have something to live in we helped each other build some boxes that people laugh at nowadays when everything's supposed to be smoothed and tight. Back then, damn it, Ross was emperor in Beaver Coulee. Now he is only king, heh, heh. Then we could live in caves like coyotes without getting either bread or coffee or other frills, and what bellies we had, heh, heh, and then Ross got himself a wife, and she wanted to shoot Fyodor and got triplets, heh, heh - well, that was back then. That was the way it was when me and Ross and that Jensen came to sunny Alberta! Heh, heh, that Jensen! There wasn't a hell of a lot of dynamite in him."

Pedersen took hold of his sides. Air was still blowing in after the amputation of those three thousand dollars. Frederik, that damned ass. A thousand, just imagine! A thousand, how extravagant that would have been. He himself had first thought about fifty but cut the amount down to thirty-five. That would have been very generous. Thirty-five, that sounded very nice. But otherwise he'd got off pretty well.

Then the whole crowd rode to a banquet at Ross Dane's.

13.

Ross shaved, cutting a couple of solid gashes. Eva gasped. She was getting her corset tightened, it was going to be first-rate. Ross happened to look at her hair. Good lord, it was gray!..and his own... He looked at himself in the mirror. He hadn't much left. It was the first time Ross Dane had thought about his hair without somebody's pulling it.

Once more he had to look over at the church. "Oh, Eva! Eva, now look - on each side out from the tower, what a sight to see, Eva - the Danish flag and Union Jack!"

- - -

At the church, between the Danish flag and Union Jack, ends the saga of Ross Dane, the Danish pioneer in Alberta.